LIFE IS DEATH

THE DEATH OF EARTH

By Nicholas Georgel

Art by Dalton Strang

Text copyright © 2015 by Nicholas Georgel
Illustrations copyright © 2015 by Dalton Strang

SUMMARY: Daichi Hara has just become a Death. With a new power and a forced quest, he must battle the powers of good and evil, save his friends, and find out the dark truth of his past.
ISBN 978-1514601211

1. Fiction 2. Science Fiction 3. Fantasy
4. Mythical 5. Thriller 6. Drama

Printed in the United States of America

First edition

CONTENTS

This book is dedicated to the dreamers who work hard to make those dreams come true.

PROLOGUE - THE HOUSE FIRE

Daichi tossed and turned in his sleep. He reached over the side of his bed as if trying to push something away, knocking his schoolbag off the nightstand. He rolled over to the center and faced the ceiling, eyelids twitching.

Images began to flash through his mind. At first, all he could see was an empty void. Then he saw it; the wisps of fire dancing, glowing like a lone torch in a dark cavern. The silence turned into the crackling of burning wood. Each crackle had a distinct ring to it, whether it was the low sizzling of the floorboards or the snaps of the ceiling trying to break away.

What frightened Daichi the most was the smell. His nose could point out each item that was burning inside, from the chemical-ridden odor of burning couch upholstery to the engulfing aroma of paint melting on the walls. But there was one smell that stood out amongst the others; something Daichi had never smelled before. It was the stench of burning flesh.

The sight of the house decaying amidst the flames was an experience that would have been emotionally devastating for anyone; let alone young, eight-year old Daichi, who could only watch and pray as the structure lurched and groaned, giving way beneath the roaring flames.

The day after the fire, Daichi returned to the house.

In some ways, seeing the charred carcass of what he used to call his home was more unsettling than seeing it on fire. Even while it was burning, he convinced himself everything would be okay. However, when he looked at what was left of the walls that used to hold up his family photos and the empty ashen void on the second floor which used to be his bedroom, where his mother would read bedtime stories to him every night, he knew that was no longer a possibility.

Daichi didn't even take notice to the neighbors surrounding the yard, or the men in blue uniforms searching the property. Most of them had inquisitive looks on their faces; puzzled as to what caused this incident.

His anguished frame of mind was suddenly interrupted when out of the corner of his eye, he saw someone running up to him. It was Mizuki Mori; the young neighbor from down the street. She was about the same age as Daichi. Her dark brown hair fluttered in the wind as she made her way past the sea of onlookers.

"Daichi!" she shouted, tears flying from her big brown eyes.

One would think seeing your best friend at a time like this would be comforting, but for Daichi, it only made him feel guilty.

Dreaming this made Daichi sweat profusely. He lurched to the side and brushed off the covers.

At the time, he didn't know how to react. But with Mori's face buried in his shirt and her arms wrapped around him, all he could do was accept her hug.

The burnt slab of wood that was once Daichi's front door creaked open and a group of police officers stepped out. They talked quietly amongst themselves, gloomy looks on their faces. One of them stopped and looked at the two children. He muttered a few words to his colleagues, then he separated himself, walking over to them both.

He was tall and broad-shouldered with a middle-aged face. Unlike the other officers, he wore a suit under a thick brown trench coat, sporting a unique detective's hat over his neatly kempt black hair. His distinct appearance marked that he was their superior, and while he had a solemn demeanor, there was a fatherly tenderness to his presence as he gazed at the two children with remorse.

"Daichi, I had no idea you were here," he said with slight urgency, patting Daichi on the shoulder. "Mizuki, I want you to take Daichi back to our house. I'll return as soon as my men are finished up here."

Mori bowed and quickly replied, "Yes, father."

Then she took Daichi by the arm and guided him toward the street.

"Come on, Daichi. I'll make you some tea when we get there."

As Mori led him away, Daichi stared back at the house.

Why should I have to leave? he wondered. *Don't I deserve to know what's going on?*

And then Daichi snapped. He scrunched his face in anger and broke away from Mori, running back toward the house.

"Daichi, what are you-" she began.

Chief Mori started walking back over to his officers; but after a couple steps, his path was suddenly blocked by Daichi, who glared at him with defiance.

"No!" Daichi shouted, clenching his fists. "This is my house! You can't force me to leave!"

Everyone stopped their conversations and glared at the boy, including Mori.

The Chief stared down at Daichi with a bewildered, yet pitiful look in his eyes.

During the baffled silence, the front door creaked open again; only it wasn't police officers who stepped out. It was the paramedics.

Through the years, Daichi gradually forgot the faces of the officers and neighbors who surrounded his house that day, but never did he forget the faces of the two paramedics. Even in his dream, their appearances remained clear as day.

The first man who stepped out was a squat man with squinted eyes; maybe in his early forties. The look on his face was grim. The second man was taller; possibly in his late twenties. A single tear trickled down his horror-stricken face; probably his first day on the job.

Between the two men was the stretcher.

Once Daichi saw the stretcher, his entire body froze as if the world had stopped. Everything and everyone around him had become irrelevant. All that mattered now was who was under that sheet.

Random murmurs were heard from the neighbors. Mori gasped and covered her mouth, while Chief Mori turned around and darted over to the paramedics.

"What the hell are you doing?" he said in a hushed tone. "I told you to wait! There are children here!"

But it was too late. Already, Chief Mori could see the horror on Daichi's face as he gaped at the stretcher with wide eyes.

Limply, Daichi reached toward the white sheet covering the body.

In his sleep, Daichi did the same.

"M-mom?" he muttered emptily.

Chief Mori twitched his eyebrows and looked

11

away.

"Get her out of here," he ordered.

Moving with haste, the paramedics carted the stretcher across the lawn toward the ambulance parked in the street. However, when they hauled it over the curb, a wheel bounced, and suddenly a hand was visible.

The sight of it was gruesome; it dangled over the side like a limp fish, charred and searing red, ridden with third degree burns. Chief Mori hoped Daichi wouldn't notice, but it was unmistakable; the hand belonged to his mother.

The image of the scorched hand burned in Daichi's head, rousing him in his sleep. Then his body lurched once more and it was over.

He fell from his bed to the floor and his eyes burst open, his mind coming back to reality. Then he rose to his feet and walked over to the window beside his bed.

It was morning, and the sunlight washed brightly over the Tokyo skyline, glistening in the windows of the immense skyscrapers. Already Daichi could see the neighbors headed for work, walking in the direction of the ever-busy Shinjuku Railway station.

Daichi rubbed his eyes and yawned. He ran his hands through his long green hair and fixed his bangs, which he parted down the middle due to his cowlick. He looked at the calendar on the wall and grumbled. It was a Thursday.

Daichi hated Thursdays. It was a Thursday when he lost his set of gardening tools. It was when most of his classes scheduled tests. However, the day he was dreaming of was also a Thursday.

This was not the first time Daichi recalled that day in his dreams. In fact, he had almost grown used to it. But Daichi did not want to dwell on such grim memories, so he began putting on his school uniform. He straightened his tie, then looked across the room and smiled.

On his dresser sat a framed picture of his mother and father standing next to each other with a young Daichi in the middle.

His mother was a fair woman of average height with long green hair just like her son. She had a warm look in her brown eyes, as if there were no other place in the world where she'd rather be. It was hard to believe the blackened piece of flesh he saw all those years ago used to be her clean, elegant hand which rested on Daichi's shoulder in the picture.

A glare of sunlight reflected upon the glass over the photo, and from where Daichi stood, the only portion the glare blocked out was his father's face.

"Good morning, mom and dad," he said to the photo, smiling.

He grabbed his bag and opened the bedroom door.

"I miss you guys."

1 — THE SHADOW OF DEATH

Daichi opened the front door and stepped outside. The sky was clear and the warmth of the morning sunlight washed over his face. At the front of the house was his garden; one of the few things that survived from the fire. There were a wide variety of flowers, ranging from white lilies to cherry blossoms, purple wisteria, and starfish-shaped pink moss.

Carrying a watering can, Daichi walked down the front steps and smiled at the colorful vegetation. His eyes fell upon a small group of bluebells near the front of the garden. Kneeling down, he grabbed a few by their stems and lowered his nose, whiffing their sweet scent.

"Ah," he exhaled. "Just like the ones father used to grow."

As he watered the garden, he noticed something lying in the dirt next to one of the lilies; something that was not supposed to be there. Seeing such a blemish ignited a fire within Daichi, causing his face to scrunch in irritation. He snatched it up and seethed, his blood boiling with fury at the sight of the hideous intruder that invaded his garden.

It was a crumpled piece of paper.

"What the hell is this?!" he roared.

He raised his hand holding the trash and shouted to the neighborhood, "Alright, which one of you bastards thought it was funny to litter on my garden?!"

"You know, Daichi," said a giggling voice behind him. "It's just a piece of paper."

Daichi turned around to a familiar sight. Mori was standing on the pathway, waiting for him whilst being amused by his rant.

Mori had matured quite a bit since they were kids. She had an attractive body; slenderly built with a full bosom, her knee-length skirt highlighting her thin legs and curved hips. Wearing her sleeves rolled up, Mori's snow-white skin shone brightly in the morning sunlight. Strands of her straight brown hair fluttered in the wind, looking clean and refreshed as ever. Beneath her big brown eyes, Mori covered her hand over the lower part of her face, hiding her cute, giggling smile.

"I swear, you overreact over the littlest things," she teased.

"I don't think you get it Mori," he said seriously as they walked down the street. "That garden was a memento from my father."

"Oh, I see."

Mori immediately regretted what she said. Once the high school was in view, she changed the subject.

"So anyways, did you study for today's test?"

"Of course I did!"

He didn't actually study.

"I mean, how hard could it be?"

Daichi sat in his desk and stared out the window. Feeling sweaty in the stuffy classroom, he loosened his tie and grunted in his seat. He sighed and looked back out the window, still wondering who littered in his garden.

His calm state of mind was suddenly interrupted when someone nudged him on the shoulder and said, "You know you're going to fail this test, right?"

Daichi frowned and turned his head. It was only his friend, Yunano Tsubaki, whose sleek, shiny black hair covered his eyebrows as he raised them at Daichi.

Tsubaki was a handsome young man of seventeen who had an adorable face that all the girls loved, with his smooth jawline and sea-gray eyes. But what drew them in the most was the solemn expression which seemed permanently glued to his face. He sat back in his chair and smiled calmly whilst twirling a pencil between two fingers.

Irritated, Daichi scowled at Tsubaki and snapped, "Shut up, smartass. Believe it or not I actually did study for this one, and I'm going to pass with flying colors."

Tsubaki frowned and shook his head. "You said the same thing last week," he muttered.

The door to the classroom opened and the teacher walked in with the tests in her hands. The room quieted as she began passing them out. Once the test was placed on Daichi's desk, he crossed his eyebrows and seized his pencil.

Tsubaki's a dumbass. I'll pass this test!

He opened his test to the first page. After glancing through the first few questions, he slammed his elbows on the desk and buried his face in his hands.

"I'm screwed," he whimpered.

He looked around to see how everyone else was doing. Mori seemed to be moving at a steady pace, and there was no uncertainty on Tsubaki's face whatsoever.

No surprise there, Daichi thought.

Then his eyes fell on one particular student; Haruka Tsukino.

To Daichi, and perhaps everyone else in the school, Haruka was the most beautiful girl in Kurosaki High. An Asian-European mix, she had a slender yet curvaceous body with a significantly large bust for a sixteen year old.

Daichi rested his chin in his hand and smiled, staring in awe at the beautiful young woman. He had been in the same class with Haruka for years, but he could never muster the courage to speak to her.

He always admired those big blue eyes of hers; so calm and focused on what she was doing. But what he loved about her most was her hair. She had long, wavy blonde hair down to her hips, and whenever Daichi passed her in the hallways, he would always catch a whiff of its vanilla scent, like a breath of fresh of air that lightened his mood every time.

Suddenly, her blue eyes glanced in his direction.

Daichi's eyes widened. He didn't expect her to look at him. In fact, this was the first time she ever acknowledged him. He tried to remain calm, but on the inside, he was panicking.

Oh no. She's looking at me! Did she notice I was staring at her? How long was I staring?

Haruka stopped writing. She placed down her pencil and turned her head, looking curiously at Daichi.

He felt as though he should respond somehow. Quickly, he forced a friendly smile.

Is she going to say something? I hope she's not mad.

But to his surprise, Haruka let out a soft giggle and blushed. Then she waved at him, smiling back.

Daichi could not believe what was happening, but he went along with it and waved.

After that, Haruka picked up her pencil and resumed her work, Daichi doing the same. However, his mind wasn't focused on the test anymore. Instead, he was rejoicing, feeling accomplished he had finally made contact with the goddess known as Haruka Tsukino.

"Tsubaki, guess what! You won't believe it! Haruka Tsukino looked at me during the test! Did you hear me, Tsubaki? She looked at ME!"

It was the end of the day. Everyone had filed out of their classrooms, and the students were grabbing their shoes from their lockers, ready to go home. Meanwhile, Daichi and Tsubaki stood next to the classroom door, and Daichi couldn't help but exclaim his excitement to his friend.

"It must be love!" he shouted, shooting his hands into the air.

A few students glanced at him oddly.

Tsubaki crossed his arms and leaned against the lockers.

"Sorry," he sneered, "but am I supposed to care?"

Daichi ignored him and continued his revelation.

"Could this be fate?" he gasped, stars in his eyes.

"Come on. Now you're just getting carried away. Listen, girls like her only date certain guys; those who are athletic, charming, and intelligent. Like me. Not that I'm interested. Anyway, the point is you have none of those traits, Daichi. Face it; you don't have a chance."

As much as Daichi hated to admit it, Tsubaki knew what he was talking about. It was known that many girls had gone out of their way to date the star point guard of the basketball team.

But Daichi had heard enough from him. Annoyed, he grabbed Tsubaki by the collar of his uniform jacket and shouted, "Don't give me that shit!" to his face.

"What?" Tsubaki sneered. "Did I hit a nerve, Mr. Sensitive?"

"Oh, I see. You just want Haruka for yourself!"

Down the hallway, Mori could hear their raised voices as she put on her shoes.

"Ugh," she groaned. "Those two are at it again."

As Mori approached them, Tsubaki continued to argue, "I'm too busy with school to be in a relationship right now. You do whatever you want. All I'm saying is you're not her type."

Before he could continue, Mori hurled her fist into Tsubaki's stomach, causing him to lose breath and fall to the ground. She did the same to Daichi, who went down even faster.

"Why do I always have to mediate the two of you this way?" she scolded, crossing her arms.

Tsubaki rose to his feet and brushed off his jacket.

"Listen Mori, if you're going to blame anyone here, blame Daichi."

He indicated where Daichi was lying on the floor, but he was not there.

"What the…?" stammered Tsubaki, darting his head. "Where'd that idiot run off to?"

Just down the hallway, the exit door was slightly open.

Daichi searched the hallways for Haruka. Ever

since his encounter with her during class, his mind was set. He was determined to meet with her in person; certain her smile meant something.

Alright; you're going to walk up to her, say hi, and ask if she's free tonight. Simple… but what if she says no? No, don't be a chicken, Daichi! You can do this!

Finally, he found her alone at her locker down the hallway, dressed in her gym clothes. As she bent over to put away her sneakers, Daichi averted his eyes and blushed.

Now was his chance. Slowly, he approached her. But before he could say anything, she stood up straight and met his eyes, smiling as if she had been expecting him.

"Hello Daichi," she said cutely.

She closed her locker and walked over to him.

"Can I ask you something?"

Daichi trembled in his shoes.

There's no way this is happening! She came to me! I don't believe it! Well come on, you idiot, say something!

"Sure," he said casually. "What is it?"

"Well, I'm not doing anything tonight, so I was wondering if you'd like to go to a karaoke club with me."

WHAT?!

He didn't think she would be the one to ask him out.

"Sure!" he said gladly. "Which club?"

"The Blue Waffle Café!"

All of Daichi's excitement vanished.

So… Haruka's that kind of girl.

Just by the name, he could guess what type of club this was going to be.

"Umm," he began, trying to come up with a friendly response. "Yeah… sorry, but, I'll have to pass. Don't want to catch syphilis, you know?"

Haruka frowned in disappointment.

"Jeez, Daichi. I was hoping you wouldn't be boring."

She picked up her schoolbag and walked away, leaving Daichi frozen in defeat.

The entrance door seemed to echo when it shut. It was quiet around the grounds of the school; so quiet, all you could hear was the stirring of the cherry blossom trees in the wind.

All the students left to go home already; save for Daichi, who was the last to leave. He hung his head and sighed as he walked down the sidewalk, the soft sound of the trees fading away behind him.

When he reached his house, he walked upstairs to his room and picked up the framed picture of his parents. He sat down on the edge of his bed.

"What do you guys think?" he asked, staring at the picture gloomily. "Should I have just said yes? Or did I do the right thing?"

A glare washed over the photo. Outside, the sun was setting. The light shining through the window cast a large shadow of Daichi on the floor.

Out of the corner of his eye, Daichi saw something move. He put down the picture, and to his horror, there was a dark figure standing in the center of the room on top of his shadow.

Daichi dropped the picture and scrambled back on his bed in fear.

Concealed in darkness, its body appeared completely black. It was bald and naked; however, there were no visible features on its body. The only exception was its cold white eyes; ominous like two headlights at the end of a dark tunnel. It was tall and slim; about six feet in height with no visible mouth. When it spoke, only its jaw moved.

"Greetings, Daichi Hara," it said.

Daichi's eyes looked like they were about to bulge out of his head. He was too scared to move, afraid it might kill him if he tried escaping. He had never seen anything like it before.

"What the hell?!" he muttered in wonder. "Is this real?"

"I assure you, Daichi Hara; I'm just as real as you."

It spoke in a serious and dignified manner; in a dark, full voice which penetrated the walls.

Daichi eased forward and sat himself on the edge of the bed.

Still unsure of what to make of this being, he asked, "Who are you? Why are you here?"

"I cannot tell you who I am. But I shall tell you this."

It raised its hand and pointed at Daichi.

"You, Daichi Hara, have the most potential. I have chosen you to become my new Death."

"Death… you mean like the Grim Reaper?"

"If that's what your culture refers to it as, then

yes."

The Shadow Man lowered his hand and stepped closer.

"The sole purpose of a Death is to save this world from overpopulation. It is a growing sickness that will one day consume this world. Right now, the estimated total of humans in this world is seven billion. Twelve years ago, the total was only six billion; and two hundred years ago, a mere one billion. This world is swarming with humans, and the Deaths exist to fix that."

"Wait, are you saying I'd have to kill people?"

"Yes. The population of this planet will never stop increasing. Life is slowly becoming scarce as, ironically, humans quickly grow. That is why I need you, Daichi Hara."

Daichi crossed his eyebrows and scowled.

"No!" he shouted. "I've heard enough."

Daichi rose to his feet and confronted the Shadow Man.

"Listen," he continued. "The population's going to increase no matter what. I don't know what it's like wherever you're from, but in this world, that's what humans do. Almost every human's dream is to get married and have children of their own; to have a family. That's just how we are."

The Shadow Man's eyes narrowed into slits.

Daichi gulped and shifted in place. He couldn't tell whether the Shadow Man was angered or impressed by what he said.

"Before you so quickly refuse, Daichi Hara, at

least let me offer my gift."

Daichi raised an eyebrow.

"What gift?"

The Shadow Man smiled.

"Immortality."

"I-immortality?"

The Shadow Man's mouth crawled back into the empty space it once was.

"Yes. Once you are made a Death, your body will no longer age. Therefore, you cannot die."

"Does this mean I'll be invincible?"

"No. Your body will still be vulnerable, but your Death powers will heal most injuries. Only those who possess the power of Death can kill you."

"So there are other Deaths then?"

"Bingo. There can only be four Deaths at a time; one for each element. In order to kill in vast amounts, a Death is given control of one of the four prime elements: Fire, Water, Earth, and Air. The Deaths then utilize their power to 'stabilize' the population. The Deaths receive more power as they kill more people, and can gain full mastery of their respective elements. Your element will be Earth."

Daichi stared tiredly. This was a lot for him to take in.

"The powers of a Death are truly limitless," the Shadow Man continued. "Tornadoes, tsunamis, forest fires, earthquakes; any natural disaster is at your disposal."

"Wait. So who are the other Deaths? What're they like?"

"NO!"

The Shadow Man began to increase in size, growing taller to the point where he almost touched the ceiling. Daichi trembled in his shoes and stumbled back. He felt like he was the smallest thing in the room compared to the god-like figure looking down on him.

"Listen to me, Daichi Hara!" boomed the Shadow Man, sounding much louder than before. "Whatever you do, DO NOT go looking for the other Deaths! They can and will kill you!"

Daichi tilted his head back and responded, "Yes sir."

Then the Shadow Man vanished. Daichi looked around; the room felt normal again. For a moment, he thought the Shadow Man had left for good. But his hopes were crushed when he heard a voice whisper into his ear.

"Now this part is important. So listen closely. As a Death, it is your duty to kill a total of one thousand people per month for the rest of your existence. Fail to meet the quota, you die. So be diligent."

A heavy silence fell upon the room.

Daichi lowered his head and muttered, "Once a Death, always a Death, huh?"

The Shadow Man nodded.

"Correct. So, are you ready?"

"Ready?" asked Daichi. "Ready for what?"

The Shadow Man pointed at Daichi's face. Sparks of green energy emitted from his fingertip, dancing like electricity.

"To become a Death."

Daichi backed away and held up his hands.

"Wait!" he protested. "I never agreed to this! Don't I have a say?!"

"Hehe," the Shadow Man chuckled, smiling his big, ferocious smile. "I never said you had a choice in the matter."

Before Daichi could attempt to escape, a jet of green energy shot from the Shadow Man's finger and struck Daichi in the face, blowing his hair back. There was a loud popping sound like a rocket exploding and the blast released a wave of energy through the air. The force of it knocked Daichi back so fast, he was knocked unconscious the moment his head hit the floor.

Everything in the room was affected by the blast. His bed tipped over and strewed about the sheets while pictures on the wall fell to the floor, shattering glass everywhere. Clouds of sawdust fluttered from the ceiling. Then there was a loud cracking sound and the floorboards broke off, jutting upward. Meanwhile, Daichi lay unconscious on the floor with cuts on his head and tears in his uniform.

The Shadow Man lowered his hand and stood there in the center of the room, unaffected by his own destruction.

Outside, the sun was more than halfway below the horizon. A large shadow crept across the floor, consuming the Shadow Man's feet. He took one last look at Daichi. Then the sun was gone, and the Shadow Man disappeared into the night.

Daichi burst open his eyes and sat up in his bed.

He immediately realized something was off. Last he remembered, everything in his room was destroyed by the Shadow Man. But when he looked around, not a single item was damaged or out of place. All his pictures were back on the wall, perfectly proportioned as if never touched, and there were no cracks anywhere. Even his furniture appeared undamaged.

"Phew," Daichi sighed in relief. "It was just a dream."

He rose from his bed and put on his school clothes, then he went to the bathroom to brush his teeth.

Jeez. That was one crazy dream last night.

While yawning in the mirror, he noticed something under his left eye. At first he thought it was a bit of dirt, but when he leaned in closer, he saw it was a mark of some sort; a small black triangle pointed downward.

Probably a prank, he thought, figuring someone drew on his face while he was asleep.

He picked up a washcloth and tried scrubbing it off with soap and water. But when he looked in the mirror, the mark was still there; no streaks or smears whatsoever. Putting it off as nothing, he grabbed his schoolbag and headed downstairs.

"No," he reassured himself. "There's no way that could have been real."

As soon as Daichi stepped out the front door, he froze in place. On the pathway stood a man he had never seen before.

He was tall and in his mid-thirties. He wore a dark, musty gray jacket with brown fleece around the collar and saggy, worn out looking jeans. He had a firm jawline with some stubble on his chin, and he had an old and stoic presence; even withered as he stared at Daichi with a tired look in his pale green eyes. He looked like a man who had been through a lot in his life, resembling an old American gangster with his slicked back brown hair and lit cigarette hanging from his mouth.

But there was one thing about the stranger that made Daichi afraid; one feature that chilled him to the bone.

Under the man's left eye were two black triangles pointed upward.

2 — FRIEND OR FOE

The man took the cigarette from his mouth and blew a puff of smoke.

"Well, welcome to the club I guess," he said in a crisp, smoky voice.

By the sound of his accent, it was clear he was American.

"Who the hell are you?" demanded Daichi.

"The name's Maddox. John Maddox. I'm the Death of Fire. It's nice to meet you, Daichi Hara."

"You're the Fire Death?! Hold on, how do you

know my name?"

Then Daichi remembered what the Shadow Man said.

Shit, he thought. *If what the Shadow Man said is true, then this guy's here to kill me!*

Without thinking, Daichi bolted past Maddox and sprinted across the yard. Once he reached the street, he ran as fast as he could toward the school.

Caught off-guard, Maddox followed Daichi out to the street and called after him.

"Hold up! Where are you going?"

But Daichi was already two blocks down.

"Why did the new Death have to be a teenager?" Maddox sighed, jogging after him.

Daichi noticed something unusual as he ran. Every time his foot made contact with the ground, he felt a vibration, growing more intense the further he ran. The shaking became so violent, it caused him to stumble. Then he tripped and fell forward, his body feeling like lead as it plummeted through the air.

When he hit the ground, a seismic wave was released. The pavement crumbled inwards and caved in where he landed, creating a giant crater in the middle of the street. From where he lay, he could hear distant crashing sounds.

Daichi opened his eyes and rose to his feet, standing in the center of the crater. He hoisted himself up the rocky wall and climbed out to look around. Through a thick cloud of dust, he could see most of the nearby houses were heavily damaged, shifted from their foundation. Shards of glass protruded from the windows, shingles were missing from rooftops, and the wall surrounding the yard closest to Daichi had collapsed, littering the sidewalk with debris of broken stone.

"Whoa," he uttered, gaping at the wreckage. "What just happened?"

Daichi felt a tingling sensation in his left arm. At first it was mild. Then it turned into a searing, throbbing pain. An aura of green energy appeared and surrounded his arm. He grabbed his wrist, but the aura just shifted up to his hand, causing his fingers to flail and contort.

His face scrunched in agony. It felt like his veins were about to explode.

"AGH!" he bellowed, sweat flying from his hair. "What the hell's going on?!"

His entire body throbbed from the inside. Grabbing his stomach, he heaved forward and coughed up blood.

Finally, Maddox arrived at the scene. His mouth dropped open and his eyes widened in horror.

"YOU IDIOT!" he shouted. "You didn't transfer your Death powers?! Dammit, we need to transfer your powers to an item right now! You have anything on you, kid?"

Through gritted teeth, Daichi lifted his head and growled, "Don't think this means I respect you or anything, but..."

He reached for his collar with his free hand and pulled out a pendant he kept hidden around his neck.

It was gold and oval shaped with a heart in the center.

"Take this," he said, handing him the pendant.

Maddox took it and leaned in closer to Daichi.

"Alright, now hold this and focus all your energy on it."

Despite his distrust, Daichi did as he said and grabbed the pendant. He closed his eyes and repeated in his mind, "Pendant, pendant."

The aura intensified around his hand, forming into a green stream of energy which swirled around his body like a tornado. Maddox backed away and gazed up as the energy lifted Daichi into the air, circling faster and faster. Finally, the swirling slowed and Daichi lowered to the ground. Once his feet made contact with the pavement, his body felt stable again. The last streams of energy surged from the triangle on his face and shot down into the pendant.

In his hand, a soft green aura surrounded the pendant. Then it faded and disappeared beneath the metal.

"Phew," Maddox sighed in relief. "Thank god you're okay."

To avoid the commotion that was to come of the incident, Daichi and Maddox returned to the house. By the time they arrived, they could hear police sirens in the distance.

Standing on the sidewalk, Daichi looked up at Maddox and asked, "Do you think they'll believe it was an earthquake?"

"Don't worry. They will."

Maddox sat down on the curb and placed a cigarette between his lips. Then he snapped his fingers and a small flame appeared from the tip of his thumb. He lit the cigarette and took a puff, as if what just happened was a normal, everyday occurrence.

Daichi sat down beside him, surprised this man, this Death, still hadn't made a move to kill him. However, when he looked into Maddox's eyes, what he saw were not the eyes of a killer. If anything, they were the eyes of a man who had witnessed too much death in his life; who longed for nothing but some peace for once.

"What is it?" said Maddox, noticing Daichi was staring at him.

"Oh, nothing."

The two stared ahead in silence.

Maddox took another puff and said, "I guess you're probably wondering what happened back there."

"Um, yeah. The Shadow Man never mentioned anything about a power transfer."

"Hmm, that's odd. Maybe he thought you didn't need it. Maybe he thought you'd be able to manage your powers on your own. Well, he was wrong on that one."

"Hey!"

Maddox chuckled.

"Basically, we have to do it because our elemental power can't be contained within our bodies. Did he mention about how only other Deaths can kill you?"

"Yeah…"

"Well, it's more that only Death *power* can kill you, which means we could accidently kill ourselves if we kept our powers stored within our bodies. So in order to keep it stabilized, we transfer our powers to an object; that way we don't have to worry about random power bursts. However, doing this means we can only use our powers when our Death item is in a close proximity. So just do what I do and keep it with you at all times."

"Gotcha. So if you're a Death, you must be immortal too, right?"

"Yup, I was made a Death when I was thirty-three; back in America in the year 1925."

"Whoa! So that means you're 123 years old?"

"Yes sir."

"Ah… so you're not going to kill me, right?"

Maddox narrowed his eyes and frowned at Daichi.

"Damn, kid! How much does it take to earn your trust? I saved your life back there, and now I'm explaining how to keep yourself from losing it! I thought you would've at least figured it out by now. I'm here to help you, Daichi."

"First, tell me how you know my name."

"I was friends with your father before he died."

This Daichi did not expect to hear.

"You were?" he asked suspiciously. "How did you know him?"

"Simple, really. He was the previous Earth Death."

At first, Daichi thought he was lying. But then he

thought back on his childhood. All the times his father took him to the forest, the garden that was so precious to him; it all made sense.

Was that why he was always so cryptic? Why I never saw him?

Numerous questions raced through his head, but his thoughts were interrupted by Maddox.

"In fact," Maddox continued, "your father was the one who gave me the item for my Death powers."

Maddox held out his hand and indicated the golden ring around his forefinger.

"It tends to work best with objects that are important to you."

"Well, that's why I chose this pendant," said Daichi, pulling the pendant from his pocket. "It was given to me by my mother before I lost her in a house fire."

"House fire?" muttered Maddox.

He looked away and zoned out, deep amidst a thought.

"Well, go on!" urged Daichi. "What was my father like?"

Maddox blinked and stared out into the distance with a nostalgic look in his eyes.

"He was a great man; very wise. Someone you could never forget."

Daichi leaned in closer.

"Anything else…?"

"Nope, that's all you need to know for now."

Daichi slouched his shoulders.

"Seriously?! That's it?"

"Yes. Right now, what you need to worry about is your duty as a Death. So far, it's clear to me that you have no idea how to use your powers. You probably don't know where to begin on how to go about your kills. So I'm going to have to train you."

Maddox rose to his feet and began walking down the sidewalk.

"Come with me," he said, indicating for Daichi to follow. "We need to get started ASAP."

But when Maddox turned around, he saw Daichi walking in the opposite direction.

"Hey!" Maddox shouted after him. "Did you hear a word I said?"

Daichi continued walking.

"I heard you," he said. "But I'm late for class. So… sorry, but that 'training' stuff will have to wait."

Maddox rolled his eyes.

"Fine, but you better not blow me off! Those people aren't going to kill themselves, you know!"

Daichi went about his day at school, not telling anyone as to why he was late that morning. It had reached the end of the day, and Daichi stood at his desk packing away his books. He looked over and saw Tsubaki doing the same a few desks behind. At the front of the room stood Mori and two other girls, both of whom Daichi didn't know. One had black hair and glasses, and the other was tall with high-lighted blonde hair. As he packed his bag, Daichi overheard what they were saying.

"Hey Mori," said the black haired girl. "Do you

want to go to a family restaurant tonight?"

"Yeah Mori," chimed the blonde haired girl. "You should come with us. It'll be fun!"

Mori smiled and shook her head.

"I'm sorry, but I can't. My curfew's a bit earlier tonight."

"Ah," nodded the black haired girl. "It must be hard being the daughter of the Tokyo Police Chief."

The two girls bid Mori goodbye and headed for the door.

"Maybe next time then," said the blonde girl on her way out.

Mori, Daichi, and Tsubaki were the only ones left in the room.

Daichi felt a hand on his shoulder and turned around. Mori was standing there, looking at him concernedly.

"Hey, you okay?" she asked. "I saw you get here late, and you haven't spoken a word since you showed up. Did something happen this morning?"

"Well, kind of. Just got up late, that's all."

As Mori looked at Daichi, her eyes fell on the triangle.

"What's this?" she asked.

"Oh, it's umm…"

"It's okay. I totally get it. It's fine if you don't want to admit you love wearing makeup."

"Hey!" boomed Daichi, puffing out his chest. "I've never worn that stuff in my life, and I don't ever plan to, okay?"

"Oh, hush you," she giggled. "Learn to take a

joke, Mr. Serious."

Behind them, Tsubaki raised his eyebrows. Meanwhile, Mori placed her hand on Daichi's cheek, rubbing her thumb over the triangle.

"Um… what are you doing?" Daichi mumbled.

"Trying to rub off your makeup, genius."

But the triangle wouldn't come off.

"Jeez, what did you use, a permanent marker?"

Daichi let out a small chuckle; so did Mori. She stopped rubbing the triangle and moved her hand away. Then they both went silent, gazing deeply into each other's eyes.

"Hey, umm," Mori began, her cheeks blushing bright red. "By the way, I was wondering if I could come over tomorrow to help you study."

"Me? Study? Since when have I needed to do that?"

"Daichi, I saw the scores for yesterday's test, and you barely passed. I'll be there tomorrow at nine, okay?"

"9 AM?! Can't I sleep in just a little?"

"Nope, we should be up bright and early!"

Tsubaki grabbed his bag and marched toward the front of the classroom with a serious expression.

"Oh, um, Tsubaki," stammered Mori. "Would you like to come over too?"

"Sorry, I can't," he snapped, turning back around. "Tomorrow's when I do my monthly run up Mount Fuji."

"Oh, that's too bad," she said, trying to sound disappointed.

Once Tsubaki left the room, Mori stared into Daichi's eyes and spoke softly, "By the way, if we finish studying by noon, I was thinking that maybe…"

Mori paused and blushed hard, seeming nervous, as if hesitant to finish the sentence.

"Maybe we could see a movie together. I mean, if you don't mind, you know. Would that be okay?"

"Sure!" Daichi smiled. "It'll be a nice break from all that studying."

"Great!" she beamed, a glimmer in her eyes. "I'll see you then!"

With that, Mori hurried off and waved goodbye. Once she was gone, Daichi sighed and scratched his head.

"Jeez," he muttered. "I've known Mori since we were kids, but she's been acting really weird around me lately."

Mori opened the entrance door and stepped outside. Several thoughts raced through her head as she walked down the street toward the setting sun in the distance.

What was that, Mizuki? You couldn't have asked with a little more confidence? Well, I guess it's too late now.

Mori crossed the street and sighed.

I've been trying to spend more time with Daichi lately… but why? We're neighbors; we see each other all the time. So why am I making such a big deal about it now?

Mori stopped walking. She was about to pass by her favorite store in the area; a small florist shop. It was a quaint little building, clearly a family-owned business, and despite its compactness, it had a colorful appearance with its wide variety of flowers on display.

A familiar scent filled her nose when she walked up to observe the plants. Pots of wisteria, pink moss, and lilies sat in the front window; just like the ones in Daichi's garden. Then she looked through the window and spotted an unusual flower she didn't recognize.

On the checkout counter sat a small bush of red Middlemist camellias, and beneath it, an advertisement read, "*Limited Offer: Newly imported from Waitanagi, New Zealand – One Middlemist Camellia bush for only 20,000 yen!*"

The flowers were bright pink in color; almost rose-like in appearance. Each flower contained a bud that puffed in the center like the top of a cupcake, surrounded by a bowl of pink petals.

Mori remembered something Daichi said a few years ago; that the Middlemist red camellia was one of the rarest flowers in the world. He said its species was completely wiped out from its origin country China, and only two were left in the world; one in a London Conservatory and one in New Zealand

Mori recalled how Daichi used to always visit this flower shop, hoping they would have it. He would go on and on about how much he and his father wished to see at least one bloom in their garden.

As soon as she remembered that, Mori did not hesitate to enter the shop and purchase the camellia bush. She walked out the door and headed home

41

with the young bush in her arms. Then she closed her eyes, holding it close like a child, and smiled.

I've known him all my life, and we've been through just about everything together. So is it so crazy for me to have feelings for him? Well, whatever happens, I know that once I give him this bush, he'll love me forever.

It was 11 AM on the following day, and Daichi sat on his front step waiting for Mori, who was supposed to have arrived two hours ago.

Where the heck is she? he wondered.

Daichi tried her cell phone, but when he called, it went straight to voicemail.

"Hmm," he muttered. "Something doesn't feel right."

He rose to his feet and headed down the sidewalk toward her house.

Maybe she forgot. I'll go over there just to make sure everything's okay.

Suddenly, he heard sirens behind him. He turned around and two police came flying down the street, lights blazing.

Daichi picked up the pace and ran. When he arrived, there were ten police cars parked in front of Mori's house. Caution tape surrounded the property, and the front yard was littered with police officers.

What the hell happened here? I hope nothing's happened to Mori! It looks like her dad called in the entire force, though. Wait, who's that talking to him?

Right at the front door stood Chief Mori, and he

was talking to none other than Maddox, who looked like he was whispering something important into the Chief's ear.

No way! What the hell is he doing here? Does he have something to do with all this? Dammit, I KNEW I COULDN'T TRUST THAT BASTARD!

3 — DETECTIVE MADDOX

Daichi hurried across the front yard, brushing past several police officers, until he reached Chief Mori and Maddox, who turned their heads with surprised expressions on their faces.

"What the hell are you doing here?!" Daichi shouted, drawing the attention of nearby officers. "Maddox, do you have something to do with this? Answer me!"

Chief Mori stepped forward and looked at Daichi seriously.

"Daichi," he whispered, "you really shouldn't be here right now. I'm sorry, but I'm going to have to ask you to leave."

"Hold up, Chief," said Maddox, placing his hand on the Chief's shoulder. "He's with me."

Chief Mori narrowed his eyes at Maddox.

"I'm sorry I didn't tell you sooner," he continued. "But Daichi is my new assistant. He'll be helping me with cases from now on."

"Daichi help with cases?" the Chief asked, raising his eyebrows. "Alright... well, I'll tell the other officers to leave. You two head inside."

Chief Mori had a well decorated, western styled house. Various pictures of his family hung on the blue walls, and the living room featured ornate furniture, including a black leather couch. The stylish essentials were mostly thanks to his high-wage position in the city.

In the living room, Daichi and Maddox sat at the dining table with cups of tea in front of them while Chief Mori stood across the table, pouring his own cup. His hands trembled, causing tea to splash over the brim.

Daichi rested his elbow on the table and scowled.

"So can somebody explain to me what's going on?" he griped. "Why is Maddox working with the TPD?"

Maddox kicked Daichi's leg under the table.

"Ow! What the hell was that for?!" asked Daichi in a hushed voice, his face up in Maddox's.

"Listen," hissed Maddox. "Just shut up and let me do the talking."

Out of the corner of his eye, Daichi saw they had caught Chief Mori's attention. He retracted himself from Maddox and sat up straight in his chair, grinning.

Maddox straightened his jacket and smiled at the Chief.

"Ah, Chief," he chuckled. "Daichi was just asking me about what types of cases I do. You mind filling him in?"

"Not at all," nodded Chief Mori. "Maddox has been working with the TPD for years. Typically, we call him in when there's a difficult case that no one else can solve. The man's a genius who can crack any case. A real modern sleuth, I must say."

The Chief placed down his cup and frowned.

"Although," he muttered, "I never expected this to happen; that he'd have to investigate the kidnapping of my own daughter."

Daichi set down his cup and leaned closer.

"What did you say?" he asked sharply.

The Chief set down his cup and looked at Daichi with a dire expression.

"Daichi," he said, "I'm sorry to tell you this, but Mizuki's been kidnapped. She disappeared last night after she came home from school, and she hasn't been seen since."

"Well then what the hell are we waiting for?!" Daichi shouted, slamming his hands on the table. "We need to find her now!"

Maddox rested his elbow on the table and agreed, "I hate to say it, but the kid's right, Chief. Now, where was your daughter last before she disappeared?"

Chief Mori nodded.

"Follow me," he said, standing up.

Daichi rose from his chair, but Maddox placed his hand on his shoulder and said, "No. I want you to stay here for this one."

"Why?" Daichi whined. "I can help too you know!"

"Yeah," added the Chief. "I don't mind if he helps."

"Normally, I'd let him," said Maddox. "But I don't think he's quite ready for this case. Besides, I'll solve this faster alone."

He squinted at Daichi accusingly.

"Free from distractions."

Maddox and Chief Mori stood in the downstairs bathroom while Daichi sat at the table drinking his tea, disappointed Maddox wouldn't let him help. From where he sat, he could see the remains of the bathroom door. It was smashed horizontally down the middle, split in half.

In the left corner of the bathroom was a shower with a sliding glass door. On the right was a sink, and on the left was a towel rack mounted on the white tiled wall.

"So let me get this straight," said Maddox. "The damage dealt to the bathroom door was by your doing?"

"Yes," the Chief confirmed.

"Chief, I need you to tell me everything you remember from last night, from the last time you saw her to when you realized she was missing."

"Well, she returned home from school yesterday at about 5 PM. A little later than usual, but not something she hasn't done before. Then later that night at about 8 PM, Mizuki went to the bathroom to take a shower. At approximately 9 PM, I had just finished analyzing my police reports when I realized she hadn't left the shower yet. Her showers are consistently twenty minutes long, so I decided to check up on her. There was no response after two minutes of knocking and calling, so I rammed my body against the door until I broke through. Upon entering, the room was empty."

"Hmm," nodded Maddox, still perusing the area. "There're no windows, and the only door to get in and out was locked at the time. So how did the culprit manage to escape?"

"That's the odd part. I'm absolutely certain no one came in. The dining table is only ten feet from the bathroom, so had someone entered, I would've noticed immediately."

Maddox looked around silently.

"Well, I have two theories," he concluded. "One is that the kidnapper entered from the outside of the house by creating a hole in wall. But that theory is impossible because if they had, you and Mizuki would have heard the sound of a power saw or whatever other tools they'd be using. Not only that, but the walls are perfectly intact. Even if they did have the proper equipment to repair the wall, it would have taken a considerable amount of time to do so. My other theory is that they dug their way in, but that's impossible as well for the same reasons."

Maddox turned his head and saw Daichi standing in the doorway.

"What about air vents?" Daichi suggested. "Maybe he crawled in through one of them."

"Nice try, genius," Maddox chuckled.

He pointed to the air vent on the ceiling.

"That air vent is only a foot wide; too small for a man to fit through."

Maddox resumed his search for any abnormalities. He sighed to himself, knowing he was getting nowhere fast. Never in all his years had he seen such a clean crime scene. There were no forced entries or signs of a struggle. It was as if there wasn't even a crime.

Then Maddox gasped, his eyes darting to the wall.

"Hey Chief," said Maddox, running his hand down the tiles. "Have your walls always been like this? Some of the tiles don't line up."

Chief Mori rubbed his chin and eyed the tiles suspiciously.

"No. In fact, I just got them redone about a month ago, so they should be perfectly straight."

"Well, I don't know how they could have done it, but it's possible that the kidnapper entered through this wall."

"What?! But how? You said yourself that was impossible!"

"I know, but this is all the evidence we have, Chief."

"If the kidnapper *did* enter through the wall, then tell me, how is it neither me nor Mizuki noticed?"

"Well, there were no audible cries of distress from Mori or signs of a struggle, so it's clear the kidnapping was carried out quickly. Two minutes at most. Now, if entering through the wall was their method of entrance, they would've had to use a tool that cuts quickly and makes no sound. But what mystifies me is how they managed to reseal the wall. To do so, they would've had to repair it entirely from the outside in less than fifty-five minutes."

Chief Mori rubbed his forehead and sighed.

"This is too much. Pass me a cigarette, Maddox."

"Sure."

Maddox reached into his pocket and grabbed a cigarette from his pack. Then he stopped and stared at the cigarette in realization.

"Wait a minute!" he exclaimed. "Chief, do you smell cigarettes in here?"

"Maddox, you smoke two packs a day. I always smell cigarettes when I'm around you."

"Not me," he grumbled. "You see, back home in America, Barlmoro was my favorite cigarette brand, so that's what you'll usually find me smoking. But now after many years of trying different brands from all over the world, I can tell the difference between them just by their scent, and this scent belongs to the Five Stars cigarette brand. It's an extremely rare brand, and the only place in Tokyo where you can find them is the Kanemochi no Hotel. I visited there once a few years ago. I remember buying a pack from their vending machine in the lobby."

"Hmm, I've never even heard of the brand. But I think I know which hotel you're talking about. The big eighty story one in downtown Shinjuku, right? I heard that hotel was bought out last week by some rich German guy."

"Wait," Maddox interrupted. "You said he was German?"

He turned to the Chief with a wild look in his eye.

"Chief," he said sharply. "Could you call the department and have one of your officers find out who the hotel was sold to?"

"Yeah, give me a second."

The Chief pulled out his cell phone and called the department.

"Hello Officer Hayashi. This is Chief Mori. I need you find out for me who bought the Kanemochi no Hotel. Text me the name once you get it."

Chief Mori hung up the phone. A minute later, he received the message.

"Got it," he said. "The hotel was sold to a Mr. Mirko Fleischer."

Maddox's jaw dropped and the cigarette in his mouth fell to the floor, his face ridden with shock.

The Chief leaned down and picked up the cigarette.

"What's the matter, Maddox?" he asked. "Do you know who this man is?"

51

"I know exactly who he is," he replied with tenseness in his voice. "And I can assure you he's our kidnapper, without a doubt. I'm sorry Chief, but I don't have time to explain. Your daughter could be in grave danger."

Maddox dashed out of the bathroom and grabbed Daichi by the arm.

"Come on," he whispered. "We're going to save Mori."

"Hold up, Maddox!" the Chief hollered, stepping out of the bathroom. "What's going on? You're not one who simply jumps to conclusions! What's your reasoning for all this?"

"Chief, this is a dangerous man we're dealing with. And believe me, there's much worse he's capable of. So if you want your daughter safe, Daichi and I must go to the hotel alone; without assistance from the police."

"What kind of reasoning is that?!" snapped Chief Mori. "And no; I won't let you go alone. This is my daughter we're talking about! If anyone should be saving her, it should be me!"

"Chief!" Maddox shouted. "You will die if you try to confront this man, and so will your daughter! And that's not a guess; that's a fact! I promise; if you leave this to us, we can get her out safe."

There was a long silence between the two men. Then Chief Mori lifted his head and spoke.

"Maddox, I deserve to know what's going on. If you do this, I'm going to dishonor our special agreement."

"So be it then."

Maddox headed toward the front door with Daichi in tow.

As they stepped through the doorway, Daichi whispered, "Cool down, you hothead."

The door shut behind them and Maddox sprinted across the front yard and down the street, Daichi following after him.

"Won't it be faster if we take a Taxi?" he shouted after Maddox.

"No!" Maddox shouted. "It's best if we run. Traffic's going to be insane once we reach the business district."

"Ugh, fine. Hey by the way, Maddox, what did Chief Mori mean by 'special agreement'? Are you up to something?"

"No, not exactly. He was just talking about what I get in return for helping the police. I'm sure you've been wondering how I go about my monthly kills."

"Hmm, now that you mention it, I have."

"Well, a few years ago, I convinced Chief Mori and the rest of the TPD to let me kill one Death Row criminal for every case I solve."

"Jeez, really?! So… how do you do it, then? You burn them to death?"

"Basically. They put them in a dark room, alone. Then they handcuff them to a chair and put a bag over their head. That's when I come in and finish the rest."

"So you act as an executioner for the police."

"Well, ever since I was made a Death, I've always

tried finding ways to use my powers for good. So I figured I might as well kill those who are going to die anyway."

"Well, I just hope you know what you're doing."

"Don't worry about me. Right now, let's worry about saving Mori."

Up ahead, Daichi and Maddox were nearing downtown Shinjuku.

Back at the Moris' house, Chief Mori sat at the table, talking on the phone with one of his officers.

"Sir," said the officer. "You sure you don't want us to assist in rescuing your daughter?"

"No," said the Chief, almost reluctantly. "I have two detectives heading to the location right now. Don't worry, Hayashi. This is something they need to do themselves."

"Well, if you're sure, sir."

"It's alright. I'm sure. Goodbye."

Chief Mori hung up the phone and sat back in his chair. He took a sip of his tea and muttered to himself, "I trust Maddox, but I still don't understand his desire to murder criminals."

4 — THE KANEMOCHI NO HOTEL

It was midday, and the streets of downtown Shinjuku were crowded with citizens. All the stores in sight were open, and the restaurants, cafes, and ramen stands were receiving the most business.

But the routine busyness of the streets was interrupted when a man and a teenage boy came sprinting down the sidewalk, brushing past several people along their trail.

Daichi grew more determined as they neared the heart of the Shinjuku district. With each step, he knew he was closer to saving Mori.

Next to him, Maddox bumped into a Ramen stand and knocked over three pots of steaming broth. The ramen vendor called after to them angrily, but they were already out of sight.

"So Maddox," said Daichi as he ran, "how did you find out who the kidnapper was? And how come you didn't want to get the police involved? Is this guy that dangerous?"

"Daichi, Mori's been kidnapped by a Death."

While still determined to save Mori, Daichi's heart dropped after hearing this.

"Once I saw the misshapen crevices in the bathroom," Maddox continued, "I had a faint suspicion that this was the work of a Death. I knew all along that the crime scene was too clean to have been carried out by a normal human."

"Hold on, even if he is a Death, why would this guy want to kidnap Mori? Is he trying to get to you? Or me? What's his deal?"

"Mirko Fleischer is a man from Berlin, Germany who was made a Death the same year as me, in 1925. He's the Water Death. But unlike me, Mirko is a ruthless man. His sole goal is to use his Death powers to take control of the world. Over the years, we Deaths have tried to suppress his spurs of random murder. I've spent years searching the globe for him, but he's always managed to evade me. Now it seems he's finally reemerged, and whatever he's planning is not going to be good. I'm still not sure why he's here in Japan, or what Mori has to do with this, but I do know how he kidnapped her."

YESTERDAY EVENING, 5:02 PM – Mori walked up the pathway to her house with the camellias stashed in her schoolbag. When she opened the door and walked inside, her father was sitting at the table with a cup of tea in his hand, police reports in front of him as usual.

"Hello father," she said, bowing her head.

"You're home a little late today, Mizuki. You stop somewhere on your way home?"

"Yeah, kind of."

"Was it Tsubaki's house, by any chance? You know, I always did like that boy. He's quite the sharp and upstanding young man. Have you ever considered dating him?"

Mori blushed and looked away.

"Um… Dad, Tsubaki and I are just friends. Besides, I don't think he likes me like that."

"Why not?" Chief Mori pressed on. "You're a kind, beautiful young woman. What in the world could he not like about you? You're intelligent, full of personality, and extremely well-rounded in the chest for your age."

"Father!" she exclaimed, covering her breasts.

"What? You think we parents don't notice these things? And hey, it's just a suggestion. You know I want what's best for my daughter. I'm sure your mother would feel the same way."

Mori was surprised. She hadn't heard him mention mother in a while.

"I know you miss her," he continued, a glint in his eyes. "But if she were here, I'm sure she'd be very proud of you. It's a tragedy she was never able to see you grow into the bright young woman you are now."

Mori stood there in silence, touched by her father's words.

"Thanks dad," she smiled.

Mori placed her bag by the door and walked upstairs to her room. Later that evening, she walked downstairs and said, "Hey dad, I'm going to take a shower, okay?"

"Okay," he replied.

Mori shut the bathroom door and locked it. Then she turned on the shower and began removing her clothes.

Meanwhile, outside amidst the darkness of the night, a man stood on their property.

He was tall and fairly built with a height of 6'3. His wavy blond hair shone dimly in the moonlight as he stood on the dewy grass which moistened his leather shoes. He was dressed simply, wearing a plain white poet shirt and dark blue jeans with no other accessories, and he had a handsome young face, no older than twenty-eight with bright blue eyes and thin eyebrows. He appeared confident, yet conceited as he stood there with his hands in his pockets and a smirk on his face.

The feature that stood out the most was the two triangle marks under his left eye. Unlike Daichi's and Maddox's, this mark featured one triangle pointed up, and next to it a triangle pointed down.

Mirko Fleischer held a lit cigarette between his lips. He took a puff, then coughed and threw the cigarette to the ground.

"Blech," he grumbled. "People actually smoke this stuff? I swear it stinks up my clothes every time."

He spoke with a German accent.

Mirko walked forward until he faced the side of the house. From where he stood, he could hear the shower running inside.

He lifted his hand and commanded, "Water Gate open."

A blue aura of energy surrounded his palm. He pressed his hand against the side of the house and there was a bright explosion of energy, the aura sparking like electricity. Beneath Mirko's hand, the material of the wall became transparent. Then he removed his hand and it was done; he had made a barrier of water.

Through the blurred ripples, Mirko checked if the coast was clear. Then he stepped through the barrier. His clothes were drenched when he came out the other side.

Well, well, thought Mirko, squeezing the water from the ends of his shirt. *Step one's complete. Now, time to get the girl.*

Through the foggy glass door of the shower, Mirko could see a silhouette of Mori's naked body.

Not bad. She does have a lovely figure. Although, I wish there was a more decent way to do this… Oh well.

Mirko slid open the shower door.

Mori closed her eyes and ran her hands through her drenched hair, washing out the shampoo. All was calm, and all she could feel was the warmth of the hot water drizzling down her body. However, Mori's relaxation was interrupted when Mirko grabbed her right arm and forced it behind her back while covering her mouth with his other hand.

Outside the bathroom, Chief Mori sipped his tea and continued to read over his police reports.

Mori attempted to make a sound, but it was no use.

"Hush now," Mirko whispered into her ear. "It's best if we don't get your father involved."

Mirko's eyes shifted to the water coming out of the shower head. He lifted his hand and shouted in a hushed voice, "Water Sphere!"

The water from the shower head shifted direction. It rushed upward and formed into a ball, floating in the air. Then Mirko shifted his gaze to Mori, and the ball shot through the air and massed itself around her head.

Mori struggled to free herself, but Mirko's grip was strong. He let go of her mouth and wrapped his arm around her stomach, pressing her back against his shirt.

She gasped for breath, but it was no use. A mass of bubbles fluttered from her mouth. Then her eyes shut and she went still.

Once Mirko saw Mori was unconscious, he released the water and it splashed onto the shower floor. Then he slid open the shower door and picked her up. As he carried her out, he grabbed a towel from the towel rack and placed it over her body.

He stepped through the barrier and stopped on the grass. Wisps of steam emanated from their bodies, fading into the night.

"Water Gate close," whispered Mirko.

The section of the wall he turned to liquid slowly reverted back to its original state. Once it had returned to normal, Mirko carried Mori off the property to his car parked down the street. He laid her down in the backseat. Then he hopped in the front and drove off.

Daichi looked stupefied once Maddox finished explaining his theory on the kidnapping.

"So you see," said Maddox, "there's no way Chief Mori or the police would believe me. But that's the most likely scenario."

Daichi crossed his eyebrows and picked up the pace, running much faster than before. He passed Maddox and sprinted further ahead.

"Hey, slow down a bit!" Maddox shouted after him. "It's too crowded! You're going to crash into someone!"

As soon as Maddox said that, Daichi rounded a corner and ran face first into someone who stepped out in front of him. The force of Daichi's speed knocked the person he hit to the ground, Daichi going down with him. Books and papers flew everywhere. Maddox ran past them and stopped to check if everything was alright.

Nearby citizens stopped to see what was going on.

"I'm sorry sir," said Daichi, lifting his head. "I didn't mean to-"

When he saw who he had run into, he stopped talking. He was surprised to see he had run into Yunano Tsubaki, but he was also disappointed. Tsubaki was the last person he wanted to get involved in all this.

Tsubaki rose to his feet and brushed off his shirt.

"Daichi?" he asked, sounding surprised. "What the hell are you doing here? And why are you in such a hurry?"

Daichi scratched his head and grinned.

"Oh… hey Tsubaki," he said conversationally. "I was just uh, looking for something. Something important… Hey wait a minute. What are you doing here? I thought you said you were taking your monthly run up to Mount Fuji today."

"Well, I was. But when I left to go this morning, I passed by Mori's house, and-"

"I see," Daichi interrupted casually, starting away. "That's too bad you couldn't go on your run. Well, it was funny seeing you here, Tsubaki, but I really got to go."

"Hold on," Tsubaki said quickly, grabbing Daichi's shoulder. "Did you see the police at Mori's house this morning?"

"Uh, no," said Daichi with slight hesitation. "I was home all morning."

"Oh. Well it looked like her father called in the entire force. I think I have a pretty good idea of what happened."

"You do?"

"Yeah; I've been looking into what's going on. After I saw the police in front of the house, I decided to visit the station. Of course, they wouldn't tell me anything, but while I was there, I overheard some officers talking about a kidnapping. Do you think it might be Mori?"

Daichi grew nervous. He didn't want to be having this conversation right now; especially not with Tsubaki. Time was of the essence.

"Don't you think you're jumping to conclusions?" Daichi suggested. "People get kidnapped all the time, Tsubaki. How can you be sure they were talking about Mori?"

Tsubaki frowned and looked away.

"I don't know," he muttered. "It's just… well, I have a bad feeling."

All of a sudden, Maddox grabbed Daichi by the arm and yanked him away.

"Quit screwing around!" he ordered. "We need to hurry!"

As they disappeared amongst the crowd, Tsubaki narrowed his eyes and rubbed his chin.

Who the hell was that? he wondered. *And where's he taking Daichi off to in such a hurry? Wait a minute. I think I've seen that man before. That's right! He was at Mori's house this morning! I saw him talking to Chief Mori and those other officers. But what's he doing here with Daichi? And what's with those triangle marks under their eyes? Is Daichi involved in all this somehow? Did he lie to me?*

Tsubaki turned around and walked in the opposite direction of where Daichi and Maddox ran off to.

"I wonder what those two are up to," he muttered.

The Kanemochi no Hotel was an immense skyscraper built in the heart of the Shinjuku business area. For years, it was one of the most popular hotels, being one of the tallest buildings in the area, consisting of eighty stories minus the lobby. But today, the hotel was quiet. No employees or guests were around. Upstairs in the penthouse, the hotel's sole guest lay asleep in the king-sized bed.

The penthouse was by far the nicest (and most expensive) room in the hotel. It took up an entire story to itself with its wide open space and high ceiling. The floor featured tiles made of glass, and underneath it housed a massive exotic aquarium. Beneath the floor, schools of various colored fish swam about.

The penthouse was most beautiful to be in at nighttime. It featured a light at the bottom of the aquarium which when turned on, gave the room a blue, ocean-like glow so you could watch the shadows of the fish dance on the walls.

An 80-inch flat screen television was mounted on the wall across from the bed, and the entire wall to the left was one giant window. From there, you could see all of Tokyo. It was quite a view to wake up to, especially for the hotel's newest guest, who was about to wake up to that view herself.

Mori opened her eyes. She didn't recognize the ceiling above her; it was far too high to be the one in her room.

"What the?" she muttered. "Where am I?"

Mori sat up and rubbed her eyes, seeing she was dressed in nothing but a white bathrobe. She rose from the bed and walked over to the window.

How the heck did I get here? she wondered, looking out at the Tokyo skyline.

Mori heard a door open behind her and the sound of people shuffling in.

"Well," said a prissy voice. "It looks like the Sleeping Bitchy has finally woken up."

Mori turned to see who was there. Standing before the doorway were three people, none of whom she recognized.

On the right stood a young woman in her twenties. She had a slender body, dressed in a skimpy black S&M-type outfit made of rubber. She wore long open-fingered gloves and tall leather boots, and she had long black hair and piercing brown eyes. She smiled snidely at Mori. Her appearance resembled that of a prostitute, but something about her seemed dark and malicious. Her name was Kasami Usui.

In the middle stood a man who was the shortest of the three. He was young; probably in his twenties. He had a short, stocky build; dressed in a plain white T-shirt with a short blue jacket over top. He wore blue shorts with rips on the bottom and a gold necklace around his neck, and he had messy black hair with scattered white highlights. He stared at Mori with wide eyes, smiling in a perverted manner. He looked like a typical street punk, giving off a creepy vibe as well. His name was Kazuo Ito.

On the left stood a man who was the tallest of the three. He appeared to be in his late twenties. He was thin, yet fairly built, and he wore a black kimono while bearing a sheathed katana on his hip. His long brown hair flowed down to his waist, and his brown eyes appeared narrow and firm, an utterly serious expression on his face. Overall, he looked like a true samurai, appearing rather stoic and leader-like, unlike the other two. His name was Ryusuke Kida.

Kasami rested her hand on her hip and spoke again.

"So boys, who's going to give the skank the news?"

"Ha!" laughed Kazuo in a snide voice. "Sleeping bitchy?! You're so lame, Kasami!"

Ryusuke looked at the two of them disapprovingly and said, "Slow down, Kasami. Let's wait for the master to arrive first. And Kazuo, quit staring with that creepy smile. It's embarrassing."

Kazuo shrugged.

"Whatever, Ryusuke. Jeez, you're so boring."

His eyes shifted to Mori's cleavage and thighs.

"I mean, look at the big picture here."

Mori blushed and covered herself with the blanket.

"Though, I guess you're right," Kazuo continued, sounding uninterested. "She probably doesn't have much to look at, anyway."

Angered by his remark, Mori grabbed a shoe lying on the floor next to the bed and threw it at Kazuo's face.

Kazuo was amidst a storm of laughter when she threw it, so he didn't even notice until it hit him in the face.

Kasami and Ryusuke stared at Mori in shock.

Kazuo fixed his hair and lifted his head. Then he stalked forward, his face brooding with rage, and growled, "You've got some nerve to throw a shoe at a Shinigami, bitch."

With unexpected swiftness, Kazuo grabbed Mori by the neck.

"In fact," he said threateningly, "let me show you exactly what a Shinigami is capable of."

Mori felt an odd sensation in her neck. She didn't understand; Kazuo wasn't squeezing her neck in the slightest, but she couldn't breathe at all. Her veins felt empty, like there wasn't any blood flowing. Then she became light-headed and drowsy, drifting in and out of consciousness.

"You know," snarled Kazuo, "most people think I'm weak and useless. They go, 'Oh, what can evaporation do?' Then they shut up... after I KILL THEM!"

Just as Mori was about to pass out, Kazuo was interrupted by a familiar voice.

"Kazuo, that's enough!"

Kazuo recognized the voice instantly. He let go of Mori's neck and whipped around. Just as he thought, Mirko was standing in the doorway.

Mori gasped for breath and refilled her lungs with air.

Kasami and Ryusuke stepped aside to let Mirko through, looking at Kazuo nervously.

"M-master Mirko," stuttered Kazuo. "You've returned."

Mirko slid his hands into his pockets and smiled.

"Indeed," he said. "I've just finished laying out the welcome mat for our guests. Now please; step away from the lady, Kazuo."

Kazuo eyed Mori for a moment. Then he backed away, rejoining Kasami and Ryusuke.

Mirko stepped forward toward Mori.

"I apologize for that," he said, as if what Kazuo did was a mere inconvenience. "They're very sensitive. Anyway, putting that behind us, allow me to welcome you to the Kanemochi no Hotel, Mizuki Mori."

At first, Mori thought these people were just a bunch of lunatics, but after seeing what Kazuo did to her, she knew this was no ordinary group of people. Around them, she felt like she was one step away from being killed. And despite his friendliness, the one who Mori feared the most was Mirko.

She looked up at him, her eyes wide with fear, and muttered, "Who… no… what are you people?! All your friend did was touch me, but I could feel my veins contorting like somebody was twisting them!"

Mirko let out a small chuckle, amused by her curiosity, and said, "It may be difficult to grasp at first, but I believe you will learn to trust what I have to say. You see, Mizuki Mori, I am a Death."

5 — A GAME OF DEATH

Daichi and Maddox stood across the street, gazing up at the immense structure that was the Kanemochi no Hotel with determined looks on their faces. The building rose so high, it looked like it was touching the clouds.

"I really hope Mori's not on the top floor," said Daichi.

"Me neither," Maddox agreed. "But even if she is, we'll just have to make it through. Now remember, we need to be extremely careful once we enter. We can't let Mirko know we're here. Got that?"

He turned to look at Daichi, but Daichi was already running across the street toward the main entrance.

"Hold on, you idiot!" Maddox shouted after him.

But it was too late. Daichi burst through the front door and shouted at the top of his lungs, "Alright Mirko, where are you hiding? Come on out and fight me like a man!"

The lobby appeared to be of high-class design, featuring tan colored walls with veins of ivory and a large, intricate fountain which sat in the center of the room upon a marble floor.

There were several plants in the room that caught Daichi's eye. In pots on both ends of the front desk were Birds of Paradise flowers; tropical South African flowers with rainbow leaves on the ends of their stems.

However, despite the apparent luxuries, the hotel did not feel welcoming in the slightest. All the lights were off, making the room appear dim and dingy.

Daichi began to pace the lobby. Then Maddox burst through the front door and stood there, eying Daichi coldly.

"What?" Daichi asked with urgency. "Are you just going to stand there or are we going to do this?"

The expression on Maddox's face didn't change in the slightest, which surprised Daichi. He expected Maddox to argue with him, or make some sort of retort, but he didn't. Instead, Maddox walked forward and stopped in front of Daichi, glaring down at him with narrowed eyes.

Daichi didn't know how to respond. Then suddenly, Maddox grabbed Daichi by his shirt and pulled him close.

"LISTEN!" Maddox yelled in his face. "For all we know, Mirko could have set up a trap right here in this room! You couldn't have waited just two seconds for me to scan the area and make sure it's safe?! Get a grip!"

"You said yourself that we needed to get to the hotel as fast as possible! I mean, aren't we wasting time?! Mori could be dead right now!"

"Hey! Who's the expert here; me or you? We need to be cautious, or else there could be some serious consequences! Do you understand?"

He let go of Daichi and stepped away. The two of them glared at each other for a moment. Then Maddox lifted his head and muttered, "If you really cared about Mori's life, you would shut up and listen to me for once."

There was a long silence. Then Daichi responded with forceful intensity, "Mori's life means more to me than you think, Maddox. And I'm going to do whatever it takes to save her, even if I have to die doing so."

Maddox's eyes rested. He stared at Daichi no longer with anger, but with surprise.

Daichi grabbed the pendant around his neck and stared at it. Then he lifted his head and spoke.

"I'll listen to you this one time, Maddox; as long as you promise to get her out safe."

Maddox's face turned serious. He looked Daichi in the eye and nodded.

Then suddenly, Maddox heard a static-filled voice from behind.

"Ah, such determination! Quite a friend you've got there, Maddox!"

Maddox whipped his head around. The voice was coming from an intercom speaker on the wall, and despite the crackles of the static, Maddox recognized the voice instantly.

Up on the 79th floor was the Hotel's security and surveillance office, and sitting in this room, speaking into the intercom microphone, was Mirko Fleischer.

The room was the size of an average hotel room. Three of the four walls were filled with computer screens. There were a total of eighty-one monitors; one for each of the hotel's eighty floors, with a separate one in the center. This screen was significantly larger, used for monitoring the lobby and the elevators. A desk was placed in front of this screen, and that was where Mirko sat. There were no lights on in the room except the glow of the monitors.

Mirko stared into the main screen, looking at Maddox, with a smug look his face. Then Mirko's eyes shifted to the boy and he raised an eyebrow.

"Who's this?" he muttered, rubbing his chin. "A friend?"

Mirko grabbed the intercom microphone from the desk and spoke into it, "You know, Maddox, there's no need to get angry at the boy. I knew you two were here the moment you stepped through that door. We

73

have cameras on every floor."

Maddox scanned the room; just as Mirko said, on the upper corner of the wall was a security camera pointed toward the main entrance.

Mirko noticed this on the screen and chuckled. Maddox was staring directly into the camera lens, as if he were looking at Mirko himself.

"Come now, Maddox," Mirko chuckled. "You didn't think I'd leave this hotel's security system to sit and gather dust now, did you? Please; you know me better than that."

Daichi looked at the camera and scowled, the anger inside him building up.

"Hey Mirko!" Maddox shouted to the camera. "Can you hear me from where you are?"

"Yes," Mirko replied. "These cameras record audio as well."

"Alright then," Maddox continued. "Let's get one thing straight, Mirko. I hate you, and I'll never forgive you for all the terrible things you've done. And I'd love nothing more than an opportunity to silence you myself!… But that's not why I'm here. All I'm here for is the girl. She is alive, right?"

"Don't worry," Mirko responded casually. "Mizuki is very much alive. However, whether or not she'll remain so depends entirely on you."

Maddox advanced toward the camera and yelled, "What's your reasoning for all this, Mirko?! Did you kidnap Mori just to lure me here? If that's the case, then here I am!"

Maddox opened his arms.

"I'm not here to play games, Mirko," he continued. "If you're doing all this just so you can fight me, why don't you release her? I'm here, so you've got want you want, don't you?"

There was a long pause. Then Mirko spoke.

"Actually Maddox, you're mistaken. If my only goal was to fight you, I would have confronted you myself. But I understand; you think I'm an unpredictable monster who does things for no reason. Well, that's where you're deduction would be wrong, *Detective* Maddox. Everything I do is for a reason, including the people I kill, or kidnap, for that matter. Now you said you're not here to play games, correct? Well on the contrary, the very reason you two are here is to play a game. A very specific game, that is."

Maddox's eyes narrowed.

"What happens if we refuse to play?" he asked.

Mirko smiled and moved the microphone closer to his mouth.

"Then the girl dies," he said.

There was a long silence. Then, all of a sudden, Mirko's seat began to vibrate. He placed his hands on the desk; it was shaking too, as if a bulldozer were approaching the security room. All the monitors became fuzzy, full of static.

Mirko rose from his chair and backed away.

What the hell is going on here? he wondered. *Is this… an earthquake?*

Downstairs in the lobby, a green aura appeared around Daichi and surrounded his body. At the same time, the floor began to rumble and shake violently.

Maddox looked over at Daichi; his eyes were shut and his fists were clenched. His teeth were gritted, and he had an angry expression on his face. The aura surrounding him spiked, glowing intensely.

The lobby suffered heavy damage from the earthquake. The pots of plants next to the front desk tipped over, and bits of rubble fluttered from the ceiling. All the cracks in the floor led to where Daichi stood.

The seismic wave released from Daichi affected not just the Kanemochi no Hotel, but all of Tokyo as well. Citizens on the street scattered in a state of panic as the tremor shook the area.

Maddox dodged one of the falling pieces of debris. Then he stopped to observe Daichi.

"What the?" he muttered to himself. "He's manipulating his powers with his emotions? But a feat like that should be impossible for him! He doesn't even have any kills! I wonder… just how much power does he have?"

Daichi stood there with his head down, the tremors surging through the floor beneath him. Then he spoke to the camera, "If you so much as lay a FINGER on her…"

He opened his eyes and lifted his head, looking directly into the camera, and shouted, "I won't hesitate to make you my first kill!"

A smile formed across Mirko's face. He picked up the microphone and said, "Ah, so you're the new Earth Death, huh? I thought I recognized you from somewhere. You're Yoshito Hara's son, aren't you? You look just like him."

Daichi's eyes narrowed and his aura spiked higher.

"So you're going to make me your first kill, huh?" Mirko continued. "Well in that case, go ahead, kid!"

He slammed his hands on the table and shouted, "Go on, I'd like to see you try! But if you want Mizuki safe so badly, why don't you just stop the earthquake? She's being held in the penthouse, which means even if you succeed in bringing down the building, you'll also succeed in killing her. And we both don't want that now, do we?"

After Mirko said that, Daichi's aura faded away. The shaking slowed and the rumbling quieted. Then his aura vanished and the tremors stopped.

Up in the security room, the monitors returned to normal.

Mirko sat in his chair and continued, "As I was saying, Maddox; you two are here to play a game, and the reward for beating this game is Mori's release. No tricks; you have my word. This is the best chance you two have. So, what do you say?"

Maddox glanced at Daichi. Then he responded, "Please give us a minute to discuss this in private."

"Of course," Mirko obliged. "Take your time."

Maddox wrapped his arm around Daichi's shoulder and turned away from the camera.

"I say we play his game," whispered Maddox.

"I don't know. Even if we beat his game, do you really believe he'll release her?"

"Listen, I know he may seem unpredictable, but trust me; Mirko's not one who goes back on his word. Of course, that doesn't mean he'll make it easy for us. I can tell he thinks we're going to lose."

"So doesn't that mean we should refuse?"

"No, you idiot; it means Mirko's full of himself. That's always been his downfall; he gives himself more credit than his enemies. That'll give us an advantage. He's making Mori the trophy because one, it forces us to play his game, and two, he doesn't think he'll have to release her because he's so certain we'll lose. And that's the flaw in his plan, because we're going to outsmart him and win."

"Now *you* sound conceded."

Maddox slapped Daichi in the back of the head.

"Hey!" Daichi bellowed. "Watch it, old man."

"That's enough. Now I say we play the game. Besides, it's our safest option. Even if we refuse and try to reach the penthouse ourselves, she'll be dead by the time we get there."

"Fine," Daichi grumbled. "But you better have a plan."

"Please," boasted Maddox as they turned to face the camera. "I'm a Detective. Give me some credit."

Mirko's voice was heard on the speaker again.

"So, I presume you've made a decision?"

"Yes," said Maddox. "We've agreed to play your game."

"*Wunderbar*," said Mirko, satisfied. "Now, I shall explain the rules of the game. The main objective is to ascend all eighty floors of this hotel. Once you make it to the penthouse, you win the game. The only way you can ascend each floor is through the elevators. Each floor has two elevators next to each other, and they can only ascend one floor at a time. In order to activate one of these elevators, you must enter the correct number on the keypad inside. For the elevator on the left, you can only enter even numbers, and for the one on the right, you can only enter odd numbers. The number entered must be a single-digit number between 0 and 9."

Maddox and Daichi looked to their left. Just as Mirko said, on the back wall next to the front desk were two elevators side by side.

"Now," Mirko continued. "78 of the 80 floors will be divided into 26 sections of three. Three floors shall equal one section. There are three correct numbers for each section; one number for each floor. So for the first floor you have a 33% chance of choosing the correct number. Then the second floor you'll have a 22% chance, and so forth. Numbers will not be repeated within a section."

"Huh," Daichi nodded. "This shouldn't be too difficult."

"There's more," said Mirko.

"Crap," Daichi grumbled, slouching his shoulders.

"Now here's the twist. After every two sections, or every six floors, the sum of all the numbers you've pressed throughout the game should equal a number that ends in 5. For example, if the numbers for the first section were 1, 5, and 9, and the second section 2, 3, and 5, you're safe because those numbers added together equal 25."

"So," Maddox inquired, "what happens if we enter an incorrect number?"

"Aha," said Mirko. "That's the big question, now isn't it? Well, even if you do enter an incorrect number, it will proceed to take you to the next floor. However, there'll be a deadly surprise for you both along the way. And don't think you'll be safe just because you're Deaths. I've devised these traps up myself, and all of them contain a portion of my powers, which means these traps can indeed kill you. The only way a Death can be killed is if they're killed by another Death. Isn't that right, Maddox?"

"Correct," Maddox replied. "You may want to keep that rule in mind yourself, Mirko."

"Pah," Mirko snorted. "Just watch yourselves you two. There are many secrets and surprises within these walls. Good luck."

The intercom clicked off on the speaker. Then there was silence. Everything seemed calm, though Daichi and Maddox could already feel the tension in the air.

Maddox pulled a cigarette from his pocket and turned to face the elevator.

"Well," he said as he lit it and took a puff, "I guess we better get rolling."

"Yeah," Daichi nodded, his face full with determination. "Let's do this."

The two stared at the elevator doors solemnly, knowing Mori's fate was in their hands now, as well as their own.

6 - ASCENSION

Daichi and Maddox stood silently in front of the two elevators, contemplating over how they should begin.

"I think we should press 1," said Daichi immediately. "It would make the most sense, considering we're on the first floor."

"Come on," snorted Maddox. "That's a stupid idea. You really think Mirko would make it that simple for us?"

"You got any better ideas? We only have a 33%

chance of getting this right, anyway."

Maddox took a puff of his cigarette.

"Alright, fine then," he conceded. "But if this doesn't work and we survive, I'm choosing the next number. Don't think I'm going to keep listening to your ideas the rest of the way."

Daichi stepped before the odd number elevator and pressed the call button. He heard the rumbling sound of an elevator approaching. Then the doors opened. Daichi and Maddox stepped inside.

It was an average-sized elevator; about $6^{1/2}$ feet from the elevator to the back wall, and $6^{1/2}$ feet from the left to the right walls. The inside featured white tiled floors and sleek wooden walls with copper railings. The ceiling had nine reflector bulbs which gave off a golden glow. To the left of the doors was a 10-digit keypad, and above the doors was a black rectangular screen.

Daichi lifted his finger and prepared to press the keypad. A drop of sweat rolled down his face. Then he took a deep breath and pressed 1.

A sharp "ding" was heard, and the screen above the door lit up with digital green letters reading, "CORRECT". After that, the doors shut and the elevator proceeded to the next floor.

"Yes!" Daichi exclaimed, pumping his fist. "I got it right!"

Maddox crossed his arms and raised an eyebrow.

"You just got lucky on that one. Keep in mind; your chances won't be as high for the next floor."

"Oh shut up. You're just pouting because I was

right for once."

"Fine," Maddox sassed. "Let's see if you can get us through the rest of this section then, genius."

For the second floor, Daichi pressed 2 and was correct. Then for the third floor he pressed 3, which was also correct, completing the first section.

The elevator stopped on the fourth floor and Maddox gaped at Daichi with his mouth open.

Daichi crossed his arms and smirked at Maddox.

"So yeah," he bragged. "Looks like I'm not so bad after all, huh? I think I'll handle the rest from here."

Daichi and Maddox exited the odd number elevator and entered the even one.

"So," Daichi continued. "If the numbers for the first section were 1, 2, and 3, I'm betting the next section will be 4, 5, and 6."

As Daichi prepared to press the button, Maddox remembered the rule Mirko spoke of and his face lit up. He realized if Daichi pressed 4, 5, and 6 for the next section, it would be incorrect because the sum equals 21.

"WAIT!" Maddox shouted. "4's not the right number, Daichi!"

But it was too late. By the time he finished his sentence, Daichi had already pressed 4 on the keypad. A "ding" was heard, and the screen read, "CORRECT".

Maddox stared unbelievably at the screen with wide eyes.

"Jeez, calm down," said Daichi, stepping out of the elevator. "It wouldn't hurt for you to have a little faith in me, Maddox."

Maddox followed Daichi out the even elevator and entered the odd, looking defeated.

"You know," Daichi went on, "if I were doing this carelessly, I would have gotten one of these wrong by now."

Daichi immediately pressed 5. A siren alarm was heard and the screen lit up with red letters reading, "INCORRECT".

The doors slammed shut and the elevator jolted, beginning its ascension.

Maddox gripped the railing and glared at Daichi.

"Good one," he scolded. "You might have just killed us by doing that."

Daichi stared at the keypad in disbelief.

Suddenly, the elevator stopped, but the doors did not open.

Unbeknownst to Daichi and Maddox, behind the elevator shaft was a small storage room which lay between the third and fourth floors, and inside was a giant fiberglass tank which contained 75,000 gallons of water.

A steel pipe connected the side of the tank to the wall. The pipe ran through the inner wall and ended at the shaft, right next to where the elevator had stopped.

When the elevator halted its course, a sensor was activated, and an extra section of pipe extended from the shaft, attaching itself to an opening on the side of the elevator. Then another sensor was activated and the tank released the water, shooting it down the pipe.

Inside the elevator, Daichi and Maddox heard a muffled gushing sound, loudening as if getting closer. Then Daichi looked down. To his horror, water was gushing into the elevator through the air vent.

The keypad made a ticking sound. Then the screen above the door started counting down from ten minutes.

"Shit," Maddox grumbled. "I'm guessing the elevator won't move again until the timer runs out."

"How much time do you think we have till it floods completely?" Daichi asked.

Maddox looked down. The water was already up past his shoes.

"A minute," he said grimly. "Maybe more, but it won't matter. We'll be dead by the time the elevator moves again anyway."

"What if we try holding our breath?"

Maddox raised his eyebrows.

"You really think you can hold your breath for nine minutes straight?"

"Um, well… no…"

"Thought so. Now come on," ordered Maddox as he ran his hands up and down the wall, trying to find something they could use as an exit. "We need to find a way out of here fast."

The water was up to their knees.

"Wait!" Daichi exclaimed, snapping his fingers. "I've got it, Maddox! Why don't you try evaporating the water with your fire powers?"

Maddox slapped his forehead.

"No, you idiot! That would just kill us quicker! With the amount of water that's in here, I'd just end up boiling it!"

Maddox had no time to spare; the water had reached their waists. He trudged over to the keypad and began pressing a series of numbers.

"Let's see," he said hurriedly. "Maybe there's some type of code that stops the elevator from flooding."

Maddox continued to enter numbers, but it was no use.

Daichi stepped next to the air vent. He could feel the water shooting against his feet like a pool jet.

Then he had an idea.

He took a deep breath and dove into the water. Then he opened his eyes and looked down. Thousands bubbles shot from the vent like bullets.

He gripped the railing with his left hand and placed his right hand over the grating of the vent. Then he closed his eyes and tried imagining what he wanted to have happen in his head. A green aura appeared and surrounded his hand.

The water in the elevator had flooded up to Maddox's neck. He kicked his feet and kept as close to the ceiling as possible.

The aura intensified, sparking like electricity. Then Daichi retracted his hand and slammed it against the grating.

The aura made a popping sound like a firecracker, and a burst of green energy surged through the grating and down the pipe. Once the energy made it past the shaft, it halted its course and shot outwards into the wall surrounding the pipe. Then the energy disappeared and the walls shook, rumbling violently. The pipe bended and contorted inwards, until finally, a section of the wall broke through the top of the pipe and crushed it.

Daichi stuck his head above the water and gasped for breath, hitting his head against the ceiling. He rubbed his temple and looked at Maddox. The water was up to his mouth, and the elevator was a foot away from being full.

"Hold on a second," Maddox gurgled. "The water stopped rising."

The water tank inside the storage room continued to pump water; however, nothing made its way through the rubble clogging the pipe. The water kept building up until finally, the tank exploded.

Maddox and Daichi heard a crashing through the wall and the sound of water gushing.

Then Maddox turned to Daichi and said, "Just what the hell did you do?"

"I dove underwater and tried using my powers to stop the flooding. Looks like it worked," Daichi chuckled.

Maddox raised his eyebrows at Daichi in disbelief.

"Well?" snickered Daichi. "Aren't you going to thank me for saving your butt?"

Maddox looked away and grumbled, "Just don't get too careless with your powers, kid. You're lucky that worked."

"Oh, okay," Daichi sassed. "So… secret code that

stops the elevator from flooding… Yeah, how'd that work out?"

Maddox twitched his lip in an irritated manner. Then he glanced at the timer on the screen above the door.

"Huh. Looks like we got eight more minutes left in here."

Daichi crossed his arms and grimaced.

"Why did I have to be stuck in here with you?" he grumbled.

Once the eight minutes had passed, the elevator proceeded onward. Streams of water spilled from the bottom edges of the elevator as it lurched up the shaft, groaning and creaking along the way.

Once it reached the fourth floor, the doors opened and the water cascaded onto the floor, carrying Daichi and Maddox along with it. The two of them splashed onto the floor like fish out of water.

Maddox pushed himself and sighed.

"I'm getting too old for this."

He reached into his coat pocket and grumbled.

"Dammit, now these cigarettes are going to taste like shit."

"Oh, stop whining," said Daichi, squeezing the water from his shirt. "Let's just get to the next floor."

Maddox slicked his hair back and stepped into the even elevator, staring firmly at the keypad.

"Alright," he said. "The correct numbers we've pressed so far are 1, 2, 3, and 4, which add to 10. Now, I'm betting 15 is the number we're trying to reach. And since 5 was wrong, the possibility of the last two numbers being 5 and 0 is out. So it must be 2 and 3."

Maddox lifted his hand and pressed 2 on the keypad.

A "ding" was heard and the screen read "CORRECT". Then the doors shut and the elevator proceeded to the fifth floor.

However, once the doors opened, Daichi and Maddox were welcomed to a strange sight.

The hallway before them was ridden with strange humanoid figures made of water. There were thirty of them facing the elevator. Their bodies were transparent and wavy with an inside full of bubbles, and they all had the same physical appearance as Mirko.

Despite they were only figures of liquid, they appeared to be conscious and self-aware. They stood tall and firm with their fists clenched, poised to attack.

Daichi and Maddox looked at the humanoids, then at each other, fully aware that these things were here to prevent them from proceeding by any means necessary.

7 — REVEALING SECRETS

Daichi and Maddox took up defensive stances against the water-composed humanoids guarding the floor.

"Jeez," marveled Maddox. "I figured Mirko could program his powers, but I didn't expect him to be capable of this."

"Wait," Daichi interjected. "Are you saying Mirko can program his powers to do things without direct control?"

"Basically. These things are Mirko's water grunts.

They're bodies of water compressed together to form three-dimensional humanoids. And he's programmed them with one mission: to kill the both of us."

A smile formed across Daichi's face.

"So they're only made of water, huh?"

Maddox raised his eyebrows. Then Daichi stepped out of the elevator and headed toward the grunts.

"Stand back, Maddox," he said, cracking his knuckles. "I'm going to turn these things into puddles."

Daichi walked forward and confronted the nearest grunt. It didn't move or react in any way. All it did was stand there and glare at him, the other grunts doing the same.

Daichi retracted his arm and a green aura appeared around his fist.

"Take this!" he shouted.

He hurtled his fist through the air and punched through the grunt's head.

The grunt still didn't react.

The aura intensified around Daichi's hand, rippling the surface of the grunt's body. Then there was a loud bang and the grunt exploded, splashing water everywhere.

"HA!" Daichi yelled, pointing at the puddle of his defeated foe. "Serves you right!"

However, his victory was soon ended when drops of water rose from the puddle and accumulated in the air, reassembling the grunt. All it took was five seconds, and the grunt was back to its original humanoid shape, as if nothing happened.

Daichi scratched the back of his head and grinned at the grunt.

Then the grunt made its move. With the gracefulness of a trained fighter, the grunt jumped and delivered a roundhouse kick to the side of Daichi's face, sending him flying through the air and into the wall.

Daichi landed with a thud and slumped onto the floor with a dazed look in his eyes.

"Wow," said Maddox. "It appears he's programmed them with martial arts techniques as well."

Maddox held out his hand and ignited a flame in his palm.

"Well, Daichi," he chuckled, "looks like that boiling the water idea of yours might come in handy after all."

Maddox punched his fists together and the flames grew larger, surrounding both hands, and he charged forward.

The grunt threw a punch, but Maddox, who anticipated the grunt to take offensive measures, dodged the attack and socked the grunt in the face with his flaming fist. The grunt's face steamed and made a hissing sound. It staggered about. Then it straightened itself and resumed its stance.

Meanwhile, the other grunts moved in on Maddox, surrounding him in a circle.

"Dammit," he grumbled. "They've figured out how to work together."

Maddox punched his fists together again. The

flames intensified, forming into fireballs. Then the grunts advanced on Maddox.

Upstairs in the penthouse, Mori sat on the bed, staring blankly at the floor. Her eyes drifted, following a school of clown fish across the aquarium.

Then the door opened and she looked up; Mirko was standing in the doorway with a smirk on his face.

"Hey," said Mori, "what was with all that shaking earlier? Was it an earthquake, or something you caused?"

Mirko chuckled.

"Well… I guess you could say it was both."

Mori blinked and shook her head.

"Whatever. So anyway, let me get this straight. You're a Death, and you have to kill one thousand people per month by using one of the four elements?"

"Bingo."

"Right… But if you're the only water Death, then who was that friend of yours who grabbed my neck? He's not a Death too, is he?"

"Oh, you mean Kazuo. He's not a Death. He's one of my Shinigami. You see, a Death can share parts of their elemental power with up to four other people. And once a Death bestows that power upon them, those people become that Death's followers, or Shinigami. The main purpose of Shinigami is for them to assist their Death in obtaining kills. Any time one of my Shinigami gets a kill, it adds to my monthly quota. So theoretically, I could meet my quota solely through my Shinigami."

"So if a Shinigami possesses Death powers, does that mean they can kill other Deaths? And if they so desired, could they rebel against their master?"

"Indeed they could. That's why it's crucial for us to be selective in choosing Shinigami. However, it's unlikely a Shinigami would be able to successfully kill a Death."

"What do you mean?"

"Shinigami are nowhere near as powerful as Deaths. One Shinigami possesses a fourth of a Death's powers, and unlike us, they're mortal. So for them to stand a chance against a Death, they'd need all four Shinigami at once. As for their powers, for example, each one of my Shinigmai possesses an attribute of my water powers. There's water manipulation, temperature, condensation, and evaporation."

"I'm guessing Kazuo controls evaporation?"

Mirko raised his eyebrows and smiled.

"My, my," he marveled. "You catch on quick. You're pretty sharp for a mere human. And may I add… quite lovely in appearance."

Mori looked away, her cheeks blushing bright red.

"What's the matter?" Mirko asked suavely. "Can't take a compliment?"

Mori looked at him again and shouted, slamming her hands on the bed, "Enough of the flattery! You know, I've asked repeatedly, and you still haven't given me an answer! Why did you kidnap me?"

Mirko closed his eyes and slid his hands into his pockets.

"It's quite simple, actually."

He opened his eyes wide and smirked.

"You're going to help me take over the world."

A chill ran through Mori's body and she eased herself back on the bed, shivering at Mirko's words.

"What was your father's slogan again?" Mirko sneered. "Oh yes, it was 'Leave no citizens behind'. If he truly stands by that statement, I'm sure he'd do anything to save a civilian hostage, especially if it's his daughter."

"But… I thought you said you weren't going to kill me."

"I'm not. But I want your father to think the opposite. Allow me to fill you in on what's at stake here, Mizuki. You see, two associates of your father are here in this hotel as we speak. They're playing a game I've set up; a game in which they're trying to reach the top floor through the elevators. But I doubt they'll last much longer."

"Associates, huh? Who are they exactly?"

"It doesn't matter," Mirko chuckled. "Because once they're dead and your father finds out, he'll lose his nerve and decide to save you himself. He'll come to the hotel alone and beg on his knees, offering to do anything as long as I don't hurt his precious daughter. Eventually, he'll attempt to strike a deal with me in exchange for your release. And I'll make a deal with him, alright. A deal for something only the Chief of Police can grant; a one-on-

one meeting with the Japanese Prime Minister. Once that's arranged and we're alone, away from his pesky bodyguards, the Prime Minister and I will have a 'friendly' discussion about politics. I'll probably torture him with a water ball first, or maybe I'll force streams of water down his lungs. Either way, I'll spare his life at the last second and start making my demands. First, I'll have him change this country by giving it the best economy possible. Then he'll give me complete control of the media, which will therefore give me control of consumers around the world. Once everyone sees how perfect Japan's economy is, other countries will realize how obsolete their current systems are. Nation by nation, they'll abandon their old ways and join us. The entire world will run under one economic system, all under my control."

Mori stared at Mirko, both frightened and overwhelmed.

"Wait," she said. "If you wanted to get to the Prime Minister, why didn't you just kidnap my father?"

Mirko sat down next to Mori and looked at her seriously.

"If your father found out what I am, it would travel up the political ladder. And I don't want all of Japan to know of my powers. *Nein*, I can't risk revealing myself again."

"Again? Are you saying you've tried taking over the world before?"

Mirko looked straight ahead and sighed, a nostalgic look in his eyes.

"I've been a Death for ninety years, Mori. Of

course I have. Last time I used a different method. I tried taking the world by force; through war. It was an event in history known as World War II."

JANUARY 30th, 1940 – SPORTPALAST, *BERLIN, GERMANY* – Thousands of German citizens were lined up outside the Berliner *Sportpalast* that night. Unlike the skating or boxing events that were typically held at this venue, tonight, *Fuhrer* Adolf Hitler was to deliver his speech for supporters of the National Socialist Party.

All the seats in the auditorium were filled. The stands were so congested, the cheering citizens stood clumped against the railing, fathers holding their children on their shoulders. The main stage was decorated with Nazi insignia. Two swastika banners hung on the wall, and between them was the *Reichsadler*; the National Eagle.

The doors beneath the golden eagle opened, and the crowd went into an uproar, chanting *"Heil"* in a continuous rhythm. Various officials of the German High Command filed out onto the stage, followed by Propaganda Minister Joseph Goebbels, who stepped up to the podium.

Goebbels stood with a dignified, yet comfortable expression as he cleared his throat, preparing to give his pre-speech address.

"Mein Fuhrer," he began. "On this evening it's not only the German people, but the whole world who listens to you. The plutocrats of the west are there again to flood the whole world with their torrent

of lies. Once more, they want to attempt with an old-tested recipe to divide the German people and separate them from you."

The crowd roared in agreement.

Meanwhile, up in one of the top sections sat a man who watched the speech from a drastically different perspective.

Mirko sat back in his seat with a calm, smug look on his face. He loved being present for the speeches. It pleased him to see such a large crowd of supporters.

Hmm, he thought. *I've run through this speech a dozen times, but I still don't know how to begin. Let me think…*

But before he knew it, Goebbels was wrapping up his speech.

"Our gratitude should not be an empty word; our gratitude is to fight and work for your great project!"

Goebbels stepped aside and the crowd chanted "*Heil*", this time more forcefully.

Mirko's eyes shifted to the main focus of everyone in the building. Beneath the golden eagle, the doors opened once more. Everyone in the hall rose to their feet and extended their right arm, saluting their beloved *Fuhrer*.

Hitler walked across the stage, moving in a stiff, precise manner, and stepped up to the podium with his hands behind his back. He stared emptily into the crowd with his cold blue eyes, frowning beneath his square mustache.

The audience went silent.

When Mirko opened his mouth from where he sat, down onstage, Hitler opened his mouth as well.

"German Comrades," muttered Mirko.

"German Comrades!" boomed Hitler in his thick Austrian accent. "Seven years is a short time span, a fraction of a single person's life; barely a second in the life of a whole people."

There was a brief silence. The audience listened intently.

Mirko smiled, pleased his opening words grabbed their attention.

Mirko carried out his speech through Hitler for the next few hours. When he neared the end, he wrapped up with a few final words.

"At the start of the eighth year of the National Socialist revolution, our hearts turn to our German people; to its future. We want to serve this future. We want to fight for it; if necessary fall. Never capitulate!"

Hitler extended his right arm and shouted, "*Deutschland, Sieg Heil!*"

"*HEIL!*" the crowd responded in unison.

Mirko sat back in his chair and sighed.

"Soft hearted fool," he scoffed, eying Hitler. "This would've been much easier had you just listened to me, Adolf."

The crowd erupted into another chorus of *heils*. Then Hitler and his guards filed out.

As the light of the auditorium faded away behind them, Hitler's lips quivered. And under his breath, he uttered so quietly not even the guards next to him could hear, "Mirko… stop this madness. Please… please…"

8 - FRANKFURT

The grunts charged at Maddox from all sides. Knowing there was no way he could take them all on, Maddox extinguished his flaming fists and opened his palm. A small flame formed in the air and spun around his index finger. Then he pointed at the ceiling and the flame swirled faster.

One of the grunts was within hitting distance. It prepared to throw a punch. Maddox opened his hand and the flame formed into a massive ring of fire which circled around his body, expanding outwards.

The grunts were lost in a sea of yellow and orange. Then the flames disappeared, leaving not a single drop of water.

"Well," chortled Maddox, brushing his hands, "looks like that's taken care of."

Daichi stood leaning against the elevator with his arms crossed.

"Hmph," he sneered. "That was almost impressive."

"Hey," said Maddox. "Don't worry about your attacks being useless. You're still learning."

Daichi snorted at his words and entered the elevator.

Maddox started the section by pressing 1, and he was correct. The doors shut and the elevator proceeded upward.

Daichi rested his back against the wall and eyed Maddox curiously.

"Hey Maddox, I've been wondering. What happened between you and Mirko?"

Maddox tensed his shoulders.

"Come on," Daichi pressed. "I know there's something you're hiding. You're telling me you hate Mirko just because he randomly kills people? No; I could see it in your eyes when you spoke to him in the lobby. He killed someone close to you, didn't he?"

Maddox lowered his head and sighed.

"Well," he began, "I first met Mirko back in 1925, along with the other two Deaths. None of us really trusted each other, but we were all aware of the job we had to do. So we made an agreement to carry out our quotas in secrecy; to keep our powers hidden from the world. I thought Mirko was an okay guy at first, until he revealed his true nature fourteen years later. That was when he started World War II; his attempt to gain control of the entire world."

Daichi widened his eyes in disbelief.

"That's right," asserted Maddox. "Hitler was not the man behind World War II. Mirko used his powers to take control of Hitler through the blood in his body, thereby giving him reign over Hitler's actions. And with that, the horrors of World War II unfolded."

There was a faint gleam in Maddox's eyes as he recounted his story, though it was not a gleam of hope, but a gleam of remorse.

Daichi listened silently to the aged man's story.

"To this day," Maddox continued, "I'm still not certain as to why he targeted the Jews. But what I am sure of is the Holocaust was Mirko's strategy to increase his kill count. He stationed himself at the IG Farben Building in Frankfurt; the headquarters of the chemical conglomerate that manufactured the Zyklon B gas used in concentration camps. Before shipment, Mirko would lace each canister with a small portion of his powers. So every time they gassed the prisoners in the camps, Mirko's kill count increased. By the time the war was over, Mirko had gained five hundred years' worth of power."

Daichi gulped.

"So what did you do?" he asked.

"I approached the situation like any other American who was willing to fight at the time. In 1942, I joined the US Army, and I was shipped overseas to Europe to assist the Western front. I participated in many battles, increasing my kill count along the way by subtly using my powers during combat. Eventually, I earned the rank of 1st Lieutenant due to what the generals called my 'unmatched skill in combat.' Word of my talents spread to the higher-ups in the US government, and soon enough, I was approached by the CIA. They offered me to become part of a top-secret special operations force; a joint collaboration between the CIA and England's MI6 known as Operation L.I.L.Y. There would only be two operatives on this team; one soldier from the US Army and one from the British Army. The US soldier was me, and the English soldier was Edmund Barkleigh, the Wind Death. Your father didn't participate in the war because he was off on his own mission at the time. As for L.I.LY, from what I could tell, the Allied Forces became suspicious of Hitler when he openly declared war on the US. That was when they suspected a third party might have been involved, and L.I.L.Y was the Allies' way to find that out. We were assigned with one mission: to eradicate the core of the National Socialist Party. In other words, to stop Mirko."

APRIL 3rd, 1945 – WEST END DISTRICT, FRANKFURT, GERMANY – It was a cloudy day in the war-torn city of Frankfurt. Over the course of the war, the various Allied bombings turned most of the city into ruins. Now the city seemed hollow. Ash and dust clouded the air as Allied troops walked down the crater-ridden streets, the musty smell of gunfire filling their noses. It was a gloomy sight. Hundreds, maybe thousands of buildings appeared either heavily damaged or reduced to rubble. Shattered glass was strewn about the pavement along with broken stone.

A small division of sixteen US Army Troops and an M4 Sherman Tank advanced down one of the streets in the West End District, headed toward the IG Farben Building. Leading the division was L.I.L.Y Operation Member Lieutenant John Maddox.

Maddox was dressed in a solid black military trench coat, featuring the Lieutenant insignia on each shoulder and a badge on his chest with the L.I.L.Y operation insignia: three triangles bound together to form one large triangle.

Maddox walked with a stern, yet uneasy look on his face.

One of the soldiers noticed this. Sgt. Horner, a handsome young soldier in his twenties, looked over at Maddox and asked, "Is something the matter, Lieutenant?"

Maddox froze in his tracks. He narrowed his eyes and stared ahead as if he spotted something, but there was nothing there. The other soldiers stopped as well.

Then Maddox dashed toward the right side of the

street and shouted, "Quick! Get behind the buildings!"

An artillery shot was heard in the distance. As the whistling sound drew closer, the troops did as Maddox said and followed him behind the building. The projectile landed fifty feet in front of the tank and exploded in the dirt. No damage was inflicted on the tank.

Half a mile down the street, in the direction they were headed, a small regiment of twelve *Wehrmacht* Soldiers were open-firing upon them with two Pak 44 Anti-Tank artillery guns.

Unless Maddox ordered the tank to reposition itself, the next shot was going to hit its target.

"Advance forward!" Maddox shouted to the tank driver.

"Lieutenant!" shouted Sgt. Horner, grabbing his shoulder. "If the tank gets any closer, those artillery guns will take it out!"

Maddox smiled calmly and said, "No, they won't."

Before anyone could respond, Maddox ran onto the street and pulled out his M1911 pistol, walking alongside the tank as it advanced.

None of the soldiers could believe what he was doing.

Up ahead, the next artillery shot was fired. As it whistled through the air, Maddox aimed his pistol and fired. The projectile exploded in midair, not making it halfway.

A *Wehrmacht* soldier looking through a pair of binoculars saw this and frowned.

"Ready the next shot!" he shouted to the artillery gun operators.

They reloaded the artillery gun and fired. Maddox fired in response, the projectile exploding halfway again.

Before entering Frankfurt, Maddox added a miniscule portion of his powers into his pistol magazines. Doing this doubled the damage capability of the bullets, giving them the explosive power of a hand grenade. It also gave Maddox the ability to detonate the 'grenade' bullets upon command, and he programmed each bullet to detonate as soon as they passed the artillery shell.

"Rifles out!" shouted one of the German soldiers.

The other soldiers, who were either camped in the street or positioned in the windows of the buildings, readied their rifles and aimed at Maddox.

"FIRE!" the same soldier shouted.

All their rifles went off at once. At the same time, Maddox raised his hand and snapped his fingers, which immediately caused all the bullets to incinerate. The only thing that hit him was a cloud of ash.

Neither the Allied soldiers nor the German soldiers could believe their eyes.

Unbeknownst to them, Maddox was using a precision technique with his powers which allowed him to incinerate any object within a fifty feet radius by snapping his fingers.

The Germans reloaded their rifles and fired intermittently.

Maddox snapped his fingers three times, incinerating the bullets again. However, this time, he felt a sharp sting in his left shoulder. He turned his head and to his surprise, his shoulder was bleeding from a bullet wound.

"Dammit," Maddox grumbled. "Where the hell's Edmund? He should be here by now."

As the fighting ensued on the street, up above, an RAF Douglas C-47 Skytrain aircraft was about to pass over the area. Typically, these planes were used to transport a number of troops. Today, however, it carried only one passenger.

Inside the plane were its crew of three; the Pilot, Co-Pilot, and Radio Operator. And sitting in one of the seats, looking out the window was Staff Sgt. Edmund Barkleigh.

He was a tall man of 6'1, and he wore a black military trench coat with the L.I.L.Y badge upon his chest. He was in his late thirties, but something about him seemed old and stoic. He had a chin beard and mustache, and straight black hair down to his neck. He had pale green eyes and sharp, stiff eyebrows. Under his left eye was a black triangle pointed upward. He had a serious look on his face as he stared out the window, watching the buildings pass by as if being carried by the wind.

"Oi!" the pilot called. "We're about to pass over the location; thirty seconds."

Edmund rose from his seat and walked over to the hatch door, only he didn't strap on a parachute. Instead, he pulled out his Sten submachine gun and opened the hatch door. He rested the gun's stock against his shoulder and aimed for the ground.

"Ten seconds!" the pilot shouted.

Edmund took a deep breath and concentrated on one area. As the plane passed over, Edmund open fired, spraying the entire magazine.

Had it been a normal person, they would've shot at nothing. But by manipulating the direction of the wind with his Death powers, Edmund was able to not only give his bullets an infinite range, but also choose their trajectories.

It happened almost instantly. As the Germans prepared their rifles, they simultaneously dropped to the ground, dead.

Even Maddox was impressed. He looked up and smiled, watching the plane circle back around.

When the plane passed over, a parachute was deployed and it fell through the air, landing five blocks ahead. Maddox started ahead in the direction of where it landed, until a familiar voice stopped him.

"Come now. Since when do I have need for a parachute?"

Maddox looked to his right. Edmund was standing on the corner of the road, smiling calmly.

In his hand, Edmund held a scythe. It had an intricate design, with a wooden shaft made from dark brown hickory, featuring unique silver symbols that wrapped toward the top.

Maddox chuckled at Edmund.

"Not bad," he said. "You even managed to kill the ones inside the building."

"Indeed. Quite an improvement in technique,

wouldn't you say? You didn't do too bad yourself, except for that bugger in your shoulder."

"Eh, it'll heal by tomorrow. Though, it would've been helpful had you gotten here sooner."

"Tell that to the pilot," Edmund responded wittily. "Though, I guess I could have made the plane go faster with my wind powers."

"Hehe, don't get too reckless now."

The Allied soldiers emerged from behind the building, running up to join Maddox and Edmund.

"Holy shit," one of the privates exclaimed to Maddox. "You're the best marksman I've ever seen!"

"Yeah!" added another private. "You blew up those rockets just by shooting 'em!"

Sgt. Horner looked at Maddox and asked, "You guys think you'll need backup? We'd be obliged to tag along if you'd like."

Maddox shook his head.

"No thanks. We should be fine the rest of the way. Just stay here and keep an eye out for any leftover krauts, alright?"

Sgt. Horner saluted his superior officer and replied, "Yes sir. Good luck."

"Same to you," said Maddox, saluting back "Just watch yourselves, alright?"

"Yes sir!" boomed the rest of the regiment.

Maddox and Edmund turned around and walked down the street. As they parted ways, Sgt. Horner took one last look at Maddox and Edmund.

"Damn," he muttered. "I've met some pretty tough fellows over the course of this war, but none of them could ever compare to these guys."

Edmund and Maddox had finally arrived at the IG Farben Building; a wide, colossal structure that served as the corporate headquarters of the IG Farben chemical conglomerate. The building was arc shaped and nine floors tall with six intersecting wings; one for each of the six companies that formed the conglomerate. Built out of concrete with a heavily windowed exterior, it had a modern appearance for its time.

The campus surrounding the building was mostly open land with a few trees. Edmund and Maddox stood at the edge of the campus, staring ahead at the ominous structure. It put a bad taste in their mouths, knowing the main weapon used to exterminate the Jews was devised here.

Edmund glared at the building and grimaced, clenching his scythe.

"This place makes me sick," he spat in disgust. "It's hard to even imagine how much darkness and despair resulted from what was made in this place. Maddox, I'd say it's about time we put an end to this devil and his bloody Reich."

Maddox nodded firmly.

"Damn straight, Edmund. That bastard truly is the lowest form of life imaginable."

Maddox's face turned somber and he lowered his head, clenching his fist.

"Dammit!" he shouted in frustration. "The Shadow Man instructed us to stabilize the population, not decimate it!"

"Actually Maddox, I've been thinking... what if we did try wiping out the entire population?"

Maddox whipped around, staring at Edmund with shocked wide eyes; then he grabbed him by the collar and shouted in his face, "Hold up! Are you saying what Mirko's doing is right?!"

"Are you daft?! That's not what I'm saying at all! Come now, Maddox, you know me. You know how much I despise him for what he's done!"

Maddox released him and stepped back, taking a breath.

"Well then what are you saying, Edmund?"

"Haven't you ever wondered what would happen if we drove humanity to extinction? There'd be no humans left for us to kill. I wonder; could that be what the Shadow Man wants? Perhaps that's our true destiny; to end the human race so the Shadow Man can start it over. And with the way the world is now, that may not be such a bad idea."

Maddox didn't know how to respond. He'd never considered that possibility before.

"Now," Edmund said forcefully, "don't you dare compare me to Mirko! I may sound like a hypocrite saying this, but I for one despise the thought of making the innocent suffer. While you and I, Maddox, must still carry out our duties as Deaths, I think we can both agree that if anyone has to die, it should be those most deserving to die. I'm not saying we're the ones meant to pass judgment, but it's the most logical option we have. It's not like we have a choice in the matter. However, if I am forced to kill the innocent, I'd give them a quick and easy passing. No warning, no wait, no suffering. A quick, clean death before they even knew what happened. It causes less heartbreak in the long run not just for the person dying, but their families also. As for Mirko, he's ripped families apart in the blink of an eye. Whether by tearing them from their homes, enslaving them in the camps, or gassing them to death, he's single-handedly caused more cruelty than anyone in the history of mankind. And the worst part is that their sacrifices were solely for Mirko's personal gain. It tears at me; knowing that their deaths were meaningless!"

Maddox rested his hand on Edmund's shoulder and looked him in the eye.

"Well let's give their lives some meaning then; by defeating the man responsible for their deaths. That way they'll be remembered not as what strengthened the Nazi Party, but what destroyed it. As long as Mirko remains alive, they'll never be avenged. So what do you say we go in there and kick some Nazi ass?"

Edmund smiled at Maddox with a glint of hope in his eyes. Then he nodded and responded firmly, "To the very end, my friend."

With that, they turned forward and began their trek across the field toward Mirko's lair.

9 —THE IG FARBEN BUILDING

SS Officers Hans Lehmann and Frederick Schwartz stood in the courtyard, guarding the main entrance of the IG Farben building; a rectangular, temple-like entranceway held up by six columns. The soldiers stood side by side before the columns armed with rifles.

Officer Lehmann was the first to catch sight of the two mysterious figures approaching.

They were dressed in black military clothing, but their insignias bore no resemblance to the *Wehrmacht* or SS.

Lehmann narrowed his eyes in suspicion.

As soon as Maddox and Edmund reached the courtyard, Lehmann stepped forward and shouted, "Halt! State your names, ranks, and where your allegiance lies. Or else we'll shoot."

Schwartz cocked his rifle and aimed at the two of them.

Neither Maddox nor Edmund uttered a word. For a moment they stood there silently. Then there was a sudden gust of wind and Edmund vanished.

"What the?!" Schwartz gasped. "Where did the other one go?!"

Schwartz felt another gust on the back of his neck. He whipped around, and to his surprise, Edmund was flying through the air behind him, his scythe raised to strike.

Schwartz let out a small gasp. Then Edmund swung his scythe and the blade pierced through Schwartz's gut. The force of the blow caused the blade jutting from Schwartz's back to pierce Lehmann as well. Edmund landed on his feet. Then he swung his scythe over his shoulder and down, carrying the two dead officers along with him, and the bodies struck the ground with the crisp sound of bones cracking.

Edmund removed his scythe from the two stacked corpses and headed inside, Maddox following behind. They stopped in the center of the entrance hall.

The hall was spacious and well-designed, featuring white marble walls and two curved staircases on either side.

Shortly after they entered, the building's security alarm went off.

Edmund readied his scythe while Maddox pulled out his pistol. Already they could hear the stomping of heavy military boots drawing near.

Beneath the IG Farben building's main basement were three sub-basements. The main basement housed synthetic oil, rubber, and methanol, while the sub-basements housed Zyklon B.

The first sub-basement was lit brightly with fixtures similar to that of a warehouse. On either side of the room were stacks of wooden crates, and in the center of the room, sitting at a table with an open crate in front of him was Mirko Fleischer.

He wore his SS uniform, sporting the rank of Major, and he held his hand above the crate, emanating a blue aura which surrounded the canisters. Once he finished, he picked up the crate and placed it with the stack on the left side of the room. Then he walked over to the right side and picked up another crate, placing it on the table.

As soon as he sat down and removed the top, the basement door burst open.

"Major Fleischer!" shouted Dr. Steiner, one of the remaining IG Farben chemists who hadn't fled Frankfurt yet. "There are intruders inside the building, and they've already killed Officers Lehmann and Schwartz!"

Mirko didn't react in any way to Steiner's words.

"Can you describe their appearances?" he asked simply.

"Well," said Steiner, "there were two men, dressed in black military coats. One had slick brown hair. The other had long black hair. One bore a gun, while the other bore a scythe."

Finally, Mirko rose from his seat.

"I see. Steiner, could you please leave the room?"

Though baffled by Mirko's reaction, Steiner responded with the *Sieg Heil* and left the room.

Alone now, Mirko began pacing the room.

Everything's falling apart now, he thought. *With Hitler hidden away in the* Fuhrerbunker, *he's become virtually useless to me now. And ever since the loss of Auschwitz, my power increase is slowly coming to a halt. I barely feel anything, now that the camps have been liberated. With the Red Army advancing from the east, and the Allies from the west, it's clear the war's over for us. Though, really it is I who has lost the war, which means I cannot proceed with this plan any further.*

Mirko stopped pacing and stared at the crates of Zyklon B, a disappointed look on his face. Then he picked up the glass of water he left on the table and took a sip.

With national control comes power.

Mirko fixed his eyes on the glass and the water began to rise. It overflowed, spilling over the rim and down Mirko's hand. Then he dropped the glass and it shattered. However, the water continued to expand, flooding the floor.

Mirko opened the door leading upstairs and stood

there, watching as the water neared the crates.

But without control, you have no power.

He then shut the door and walked upstairs.

In twenty minutes, all three sub-basements were flooded.

Maddox and Edmund stood back to back in the entrance hall with their weapons raised. The sounds of the approaching soldiers drew close. Then finally, a swarm of SS guards rushed in from the left and right corridors and stopped on the steps, setting up a formation.

Maddox and Edmund were surrounded on all sides. The SS guards aimed their rifles, prepared to fire, until suddenly both sides were interrupted by a familiar voice on the intercom.

"HALT!" the voice shouted. "Nobody make a move."

A spark of rage flared within Edmund and Maddox upon hearing Mirko's voice.

"Now listen," Mirko continued. "These men before you are guests of mine, so I don't want anyone to so much as lay a finger on them. And since we have some catching up to do, I want all personnel to evacuate at once. Anyone who stays behind will be shot. Thank you."

The intercom clicked off, leaving Maddox, Edmund, and the Nazi soldiers standing there awkwardly. A few soldiers formed into huddles.

"I sure hope Major Fleischer knows what he's doing," murmured one soldier.

"What the hell was the *Fuhrer* thinking?" griped the soldier next to him. "Putting a man like him in charge of IG Farben?"

One of the senior officers overheard their conversation and said, "Whatever he was thinking, it doesn't matter now. The *Fuhrer's* holed up in the *Fuhrerbunker* with the rest of the nation's leaders, and the Allies are advancing into the heart of Germany; into this very city. With all that's going on, maybe running away is our best option."

In the next few minutes, the SS soldiers and IG Farben chemists proceeded to exit the building, dispersing across the grounds into the streets of Frankfurt. Some divided themselves into regiments, choosing to fight the allied forces that lay within the city.

As soon as the building was empty, Maddox and Edmund proceeded down the corridor, the tension growing with each passing door. Then finally, they reached a large steel door labeled, *"Laboratory 1: Zyklon B"*.

Maddox glanced at Edmund and nodded. Edmund did the same.

When Edmund grabbed the door handle, he could already feel the bloodlust of his enemy oozing through the cold metal. Carefully, he opened the door.

The laboratory was about the size of a cafeteria, featuring six long metal tables cluttered with various chemistry materials, including beakers, test tubes, and chemical containers. Against the wall on the left were three cylindrical chemical vats containing hydrogen cyanide, the main base used to make Zyklon B. On the right were another three vats containing ethyl bromoacetate, a toxic compound. On the wall in the back were four large windows, all which were open for ventilation. And standing in the center of the room, with a smirk on his face and his arms extended in a welcoming manner, was Mirko Fleischer.

"Welcome, my fellow Deaths," he said. "My, my, it's been quite a while, hasn't it? You both look well. Of course, still the same as twenty years ago. John Maddox, the brilliant detective himself who spends as much time solving cases as he does smoke his cigarettes. And Edmund Barkleigh, the ex-aristocrat who despises corruption of power; who cares for his people more than himself, you truly are unique. Your curious, intuitive thoughts on humanity have always fascinated me. So anyway, my dear friends, what brings you to the IG Farben Headquarters today?"

"Shut it," snapped Edmund. "You know exactly why we're here, Mirko."

"Hmm," Mirko rubbed his chin. "Perhaps you two are short on kills? If either of you are feeling needy, I have well over three hundred men outside. Please, take whomever you'd like. They're of no use to me now."

Maddox narrowed his eyes and said, "I'm sure they're not. The war's over for you now, Mirko. The

Allied forces have taken the city. Pretty soon, you'll have no one left in the Reich to rely on. Not even the *Fuhrer*."

Mirko frowned slightly, his face turning somber.

"Maddox, I've been thinking the exact same thing. Lately, Adolf's become more difficult to control. It seems he's found a way to fight my power. After being confined for such a long time, it doesn't surprise me. However, if he keeps this up any longer, he'll eventually regain control of himself. And if that happens, he'll reveal my secrets. Aside from you two, he's the only person who knows what I am truly capable of. Therefore, I have no choice but to dispose of him."

Edmund gritted his teeth. Mirko grinned.

"It's only a matter of time," he continued. "I'll wait until the opportune moment. That's when I'll force him to take his own life. Maybe he'll poison himself, maybe he'll hold a gun to his head; I don't know. But soon, the Third Reich's beloved leader will become a piece of history, left with a legacy that will remember him as one of the world's greatest monsters. Such a shame; he had so much potential. Though, I should've known I wouldn't be able to trust him in carrying out my master plan."

"And what plan would that be?" asked Maddox.

Mirko closed his eyes and sighed.

"Well, I guess there's no point in hiding it. You see, my intention for Zyklon B wasn't just to use it for the camps. What I really wanted was to build up the IG Farben Corporation so it could make enough

Zyklon B for military purposes. I planned to take over the world by using this gas. Just imagine; a single regiment gassing an entire city. That's all it would take. But it doesn't matter now; I've given up on that plan."

"You're lying," said Edmund.

"No," said Mirko firmly. "I'm not. As soon as I found out you were here, I flooded all the basements that housed Zyklon B. You can see for yourselves if you'd like. Though, I wouldn't recommend it. By now, the water's probably toxic enough to kill you."

Suddenly, Mirko grunted in pain and grabbed his forehead, stumbling in place.

"Ach," he grunted. "Adolf's putting up quite a fight. But no matter; I'll put him out of his misery soon enough."

And with that, Edmund snapped.

"You bastard!" he shouted, his voice full with rage. "Men like you disgust me! You take advantage of power and use it solely for your benefit! All these years, you've cowardly hid behind a man who would've made a great leader, and now he'll only be remembered as a cruel and ruthless dictator!"

A gust of wind swept through the room and Edmund vanished. Then Mirko looked up; Edmund was plummeting downward above his head, his scythe ready to swing.

"And for that," Edmund shouted, "you must pay with your life!"

Just before Edmund could pierce his blade through Mirko's head, Mirko vanished and appeared in the air above Edmund.

Edmund looked up and gasped.

Then Mirko extended his arms and the water in the beakers flew into the air, gathering in Mirko's hands.

Mirko shot the water down on Edmund like a jet, massing a water ball around him.

Edmund didn't move or struggle, but once Mirko finished forming the water ball, Edmund swung his scythe sideways and a gust of wind was released, causing the water to splash everywhere.

As Edmund and Mirko landed on the floor, Maddox's eyes darted to the table on his right, where a large container with a flammable symbol sat. Maddox picked up the container, opened it, and threw it at Mirko. Then he snapped his fingers and shot a single flame.

The granulated chemicals spilled from the container and surrounded Mirko in the air. Then the flame hit the chemicals and there was a massive explosion, engulfing the laboratory in flames.

Edmund was unscathed from the explosion, but Mirko had disappeared. He stumbled back. Then he heard a loud creaking from above and he looked up; the ceiling was crumbling apart from the explosion. It lurched once more; then it caved in.

Edmund had nowhere to run. All he could do was stand there as the planks of wood and metal came crashing down on him.

The debris landed with a loud crash, crushing two of the tables in the center of the room, releasing a thick cloud of dust.

"Edmund!" shouted Maddox, darting through the dust and smoke.

Edmund lay with his torso protruding from beneath the wreckage, a defeated look on his face. Maddox stuck his hands under the planks of wood and tried lifting the debris.

"Dammit!" he grunted. "It's too heavy!"

"Don't worry about me, Maddox. You need to save yourself right now. The fire's spreading fast; once it reaches those hydrogen cyanide tanks, it'll kill the both of us."

"Don't worry, Edmund," Maddox reassured, raising his hands at the flames. "Have you forgotten? I'm a fire Death."

A red aura appeared around his hands. Then he closed his eyes and lowered his arms, expecting the flames to lower with them. However, when he opened his eyes, the fire appeared unaffected. Confused, Maddox flailed his arms about, hoping the flames would respond in some way, but all they did was bend toward the sides.

"What the hell?" Maddox exclaimed. "I can't put it out! Hell, I'm barely moving it!"

"That's because it's a chemical fire, Maddox."

Maddox whipped around, only to find Mirko standing in one of the windows on the back wall with a smirk on his face, his hand gripped to a dangling rope ladder.

Outside, a zeppelin hovered above the IG Farben building.

The airship was gargantuan in size; larger than the IG Farben building itself. Each of its tails featured a swastika, and on its side, it bore the name, *LZ-131 Fleischer.*

Inside the building, Maddox could hear the humming of its propellers.

"Are you insane?!" he shouted at Mirko. "You ordered a zeppelin to rescue you from a chemical fire?! And wait a minute; I thought Germany scrapped those years ago."

Mirko stepped one foot on the ladder and chuckled.

"Oh yes, and the Nazis have *never* lied before. And for your information, Maddox, the only problem my zeppelins have with fire is you. Don't think I don't know who caused the *Hindenburg* fire."

"Hey, I was in New Jersey at the time and I was short on kills."

Edmund turned his head at Mirko.

"Hey you bastard!" he shouted. "What have you done to the flames? Why don't Maddox's powers have any effect?"

"Don't be angry at me, Edmund. After all, Maddox is the one who got you into this mess. It's quite simple, really. A chemical fire is water-based; so in this case, I'm in control of the flames."

Mirko tugged on the rope three times and latched himself onto the ladder. Then, responding to Mirko's request, the zeppelin rose into the air and set course straight ahead.

Slowly, the IG Farben building became smaller in

the distance, smoke from the fire blackening the sky.

"How ironic," Mirko muttered. "I've harnessed Maddox's power, and in turn it will take his life. As for Edmund, I hope he suffers. But I hope he doesn't die."

The *Fleischer* ascended into the clouds. Hidden from the allies down below, the airborne giant continued its course eastbound, heading out of the city, and soon, out of Germany.

10 — A GUST OF WIND

The fire raged on inside the laboratory. Several more small explosions followed as the fire spread toward the open chemicals on the tables. The walls creaked and groaned, showing signs the room was about to collapse.

Maddox stood there motionless as he stared into the mass of flames.

How embarrassing, he thought, a frustrated look on his face. *I can't even control my own element. It's as if I'm powerless... No. Now's not the time to think like that.*

I have to save Edmund!

Desperately, Maddox waved his arms, managing to move a few of the flames away. However, his attempts were futile. They were surrounded on all sides by an incoming sea of fire.

"It's no use," said Edmund grimly. "Don't worry about me, Maddox. Get yourself out of here and go after Mirko. Our mission comes first."

"Don't talk like that!" Maddox shouted. "We're in this together; to the end! I'm not leaving you behind!"

Out of the corner of his eye, Maddox caught sight of the flames surrounding the HCN tanks. He gasped under his breath and raised his hand once more.

"Maddox," said Edmund calmly. "Stop. It's not your time yet."

Maddox stopped fighting the flames and turned his head. Edmund smiled faintly.

"So smoke a good one for me."

Edmund lifted his hand and a white aura appeared in his palm.

"I'm sorry," he said. "I can't make it. Goodbye, Maddox."

A spiraling blast of wind shot from his hand, sending Maddox flying through the air and out the window.

"EDMUND!" shouted Maddox as the wind carried him away.

"Live on for me," muttered Edmund.

Finally, the fire melted through the metal of the

vat, causing the hydrogen cyanide to combust.

As soon as Maddox passed through the window frame, the explosion occurred inside, and Edmund's face was lost beneath the flames, along with the rest of the laboratory. Fire and smoke burst through the windows, nearly singeing Maddox's clothes.

The wind carried Maddox into a tree. He crashed through its branches and tumbled to the ground.

Maddox landed on his backside and clutched his left shoulder, grunting in pain. Then, using his uninjured arm, he pushed himself up and stared mournfully at the blazing windows of the IG Farben building.

"Why, Edmund?" he muttered. "Why'd you save me, dammit?"

He lowered his head and rose to his feet.

"I promise you, Edmund. Neither you nor anyone else will be remembered in vain. I swear on the blood of all the people I've killed; I'll stop at nothing to put an end to Mirko. No matter how long it takes me, even if I have to search this entire earth, I swear I'll make him pay."

Trudging along, Maddox walked across the grounds and disappeared into the streets of Frankfurt.

Daichi stared unbelievably at Maddox once he finished recounting the story.

"Operation L.I.L.Y was both a success and failure," Maddox continued. "We succeeded in forcing Mirko to surrender, but we didn't succeed in capturing or killing him. After the incident, General Eisenhower and the allies repaired the IG Farben building and made it the Allied Command's supreme headquarters. As for Edmund, they buried his remains at a cemetery in Frankfurt. I was there for his funeral along with most of the Allied Command, and we made sure to give him a proper sendoff. As for Mirko, the allies never found him. A month later, Hitler was found dead in the *Fuhrerbunker*. And by then, I was the only one left; the only one who knew of the true *Fuhrer*."

Daichi frowned and stared solemnly at the floor.

"Don't be afraid," Maddox reassured. "I won't force you to fight Mirko. Just leave him to me."

He lifted his finger to press the next number on the keypad.

"I'm not afraid!" Daichi shouted.

Maddox whipped around in alarm.

Daichi stood with his head down and his fists clenched.

"I'm not afraid to fight him," he muttered. "I don't care if you think I'm weak. It's just like you said; we're here to save Mori. And that's exactly what I'm going to do! Don't expect me to hold back, though; because whatever the risk, whatever it takes, I'll fight Mirko to the death, so no one will ever have to suffer his cruelty again!"

Daichi paused. He lifted his head and looked at Maddox no longer with fear, but with determination, a single tear trickling down his face.

"I don't care if it costs me my life," he continued,

"because Mori's life is worth more than me killing people in order to survive. So what do you say, Maddox? Let's both go up there and defeat Mirko. We'll fulfill that promise together; for Edmund's sake."

Maddox smiled with a glint of admiration in his eyes. He placed his hand on Daichi's shoulder and said, "If there's anything I learned from my years in the military, it's that fighting's not just about strength. It's about having heart, and the courage to push on."

Daichi smiled and nodded firmly.

"Alright," said Maddox, cracking his knuckles. "Now let's go kick that bastard's ass."

He turned around and pressed the next number on the keypad without hesitation. The screen above the door read, "CORRECT."

Daichi leaned against the wall and let Maddox press the numbers for the next four sections, getting all of them correct.

It was at floor 42 when Daichi decided to look over and see what numbers Maddox was pressing. To his surprise, Maddox was pressing the same numbers as he did the last section.

"Um… Maddox," said Daichi, "have you been pressing the same numbers for every two sections?"

"Oh… shit. Indeed I have. I guess I didn't realize it. Wait a minute, Daichi. That's it!"

"What's it?"

"You've solved the puzzle! With the exception of the first two sections, for every two sections afterwards, the numbers I've been pressing are 1, 2,

3, 7, 8, and 9. Those numbers add to 30. For floors 1 through 6, our sum was 15, and since 30 plus 15 equals 45, we were safe. The pattern's simple, since it just keeps adding 30 on top of the original 15. I bet those traps were meant to distract us so we'd lose track of the pattern. However, at floor 78, the pattern ends, which means Mirko has something in store for us on the 79th floor."

Maddox turned and pressed 1 on the keypad, the screen dinging correct.

"Well," he sighed. "I guess it's small potatoes for us until then."

Daichi stared at Maddox with a dumbfounded look on his face.

"Wait!" he interjected. "You zoned out the whole time you were telling the story?! You could have killed us!"

"Oh please, you're telling me you've *never* zoned before?"

Daichi opened his mouth to speak; then he shut it and leaned against the wall, knowing he had lost the argument.

As the elevator made its way up the hotel, upstairs in the security room, Mirko sat in his chair watching the main computer screen.

There was a layout of the floors onscreen; whatever floor the elevator was on, the floor number would blink, and to Mirko's disappointment, the elevator was nearing the penthouse.

Mirko leaned forward in his chair and narrowed

his eyes.

Well, well. They managed to figure out the puzzle. Looks like I'm going to have to speed up preparations for the final stage…

Mirko turned his chair and looked at the open doorway behind him.

"Kasami…" he said.

A cloud of steam massed in the doorway.

"Yes?" said a woman's voice.

"Our guests will be arriving after all. Please give them a warm welcome."

Kasami stepped through the steam and sniggered.

"Ooh, this should be fun."

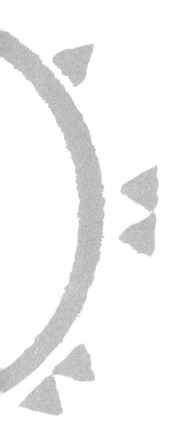

11 — FREEZING POINT

The elevator finally made it to floor seventy-eight. Maddox took a deep breath and pressed 9, the last number of the puzzle, and the elevator proceeded.

"We have two options once we reach the next floor," Maddox explained. "Depending on what obstacle awaits us, we could either fight it together or split up."

"I say we fight it together," said Daichi immediately. "I mean, I want to have at Mirko too."

"I get that. But we need to save Mori as quickly

135

as possible. If you stay behind and fight whatever's on the seventy-ninth floor, I can get a head start on fighting Mirko in the penthouse."

"How about you stay behind and I fight Mirko?"

"No. Listen, whether or not you care what I have to say, you need to face the facts. Mirko has a six-million kill count in his pocket; you on the other hand have no kills to back up your power. You can't win against him. I know how much you want to save Mori, but if you lose and die, it won't help her much."

Daichi looked away. Despite his disappointment, he knew Maddox was right.

"Fine," he grumbled.

The elevator doors opened; they had reached floor seventy-nine.

Maddox scanned the hallway before stepping out of the elevator. The hallway was empty, aside from a table next to the wall with a pot of red flowers on it.

Daichi's face lit up.

"No way!" he gasped. "How in the world did this hotel come by those?"

He dashed out of the elevator and kneeled in front of the table, observing the flowers intently.

"Be careful!" cautioned Maddox. "It might be a trap. For all we know, those flowers could be toxic."

At the end of the hallway, Maddox's warning was responded by an unfamiliar voice.

"Don't worry… they're not toxic."

Not a moment later, Kasami stepped out from behind the doorway and leaned against the wall, posed provocatively.

"That's right," nodded Daichi, unaware of Kasami. "These are Middlemist Red Camellias; one of the world's rarest flowers. My father and I spent years searching flower shops for these, but we could never get our hands on them. We would've killed to see at least one bloom in our garden."

Kasami narrowed her eyes and smirked.

"So, you like them, huh?" she sneered.

Kasami extended her arm and opened her palm, emitting a cloud of hot steam. Then with the swift motion of her hand, she shot the steam at the flower pot.

Daichi whipped around just in time to react. He pulled his hand from the incoming steam and leapt back. After the wisps cleared away, his heart dropped.

He stared with wide eyes, his face ridden with horror at the tragic sight of the camellias drooped over the side, their petals shriveled and devoid of color.

Kasami snickered and walked over to Daichi.

"Aw, what's the matter?" she taunted. "You gonna cry over some stupid flowers?"

"Just who the hell are you?" asked Daichi, raising his voice.

"Kasami Usui. I'm one of Mirko's Shinigami."

Daichi turned his head and raised an eyebrow at her.

"A Shinigami?" he asked incredulously. "What do you mean?"

"Ah," she nodded, raising her eyebrows. "Maddox is still keeping secrets from you, I see. But don't worry. You'll find out soon enough, once I kill you."

"You shut up!" Maddox shouted.

"What's she talking about, Maddox?" asked Daichi, eying Maddox suspiciously. "Are you hiding something from me?"

"No," he responded. "I was never trying to keep secrets from you, Daichi. I just didn't tell you about Shinigami because I wasn't aware Mirko recruited any. I can explain better later, but right now, all you need to know is that she has water powers like Mirko. Though, she's nowhere near as powerful."

Kasami scowled, giving Maddox a dirty look.

"But don't worry," Maddox reassured.

He walked over and positioned himself next to Daichi.

"We can defeat her together."

"No," Daichi objected, stepping in front of Maddox. "She's mine to fight."

"You sure?" he asked.

"Yeah, you go on ahead. I'll catch up. But first, I need to teach this bitch a lesson."

"Ooh," Kasami sneered. "I like men who talk big. Killing you will be fun!"

Maddox nodded to Daichi and headed down the hallway. He entered through the doorway; on his left was a flight of stairs which led to the penthouse.

As Maddox ran up the stairs, he thought to himself.

Letting Daichi fight Kasami alone was probably a bad

idea, considering he still has much to learn about his powers. But there's no point in turning back now. Once Daichi's made up his mind, there's no changing it.

Daichi confronted Kasami in the hallway and raised his fists, preparing to fight. Kasami crossed her arms and laughed.

"I knew the Tokyo Police Department was low on funds, but to send a kid is just pitiful!"

With that, Daichi made the first move by throwing a punch at Kasami. However, just as he was about to hit her face, a cloud of steam appeared before him and he swung through the steam, hitting nothing.

The steam surrounded him on all sides in a circular wall. He turned around, expecting to see Kasami, but she was nowhere to be seen.

Outside the steam cloud, Kasami watched as Daichi's shadow moved about helplessly. Then she held out her hand and whispered, "Water freeze."

An ice spear formed in her hand. Once it solidified, Kasami leapt through the steam, poised to strike.

Daichi heard movement from behind and whipped around just as Kasami passed through the steam. She thrust the spear at his heart and he dodged to the side, managing to avoid impalement. However, the tip of the spear caught a bit of skin. There was a fierce stinging and a flash of red.

Daichi grunted in pain and clutched his left shoulder. Then, in his anger, he swung his fist at Kasami and she backed away, dodging the attack. But Daichi continued the offense. He jumped in the air and attempted a high roundhouse kick, but with impressive flexibility, she bent backwards and avoided it.

"Oh Daichi," she sighed, straightening herself. "Speed that slow won't get you anywhere…"

Snorting at her words, Daichi hurled his fist at Kasami face. She caught it as if it were nothing.

"Except in bed," she winked.

Kasami released his hand then delivered an upward front kick to his face. Her foot made contact with Daichi's right cheek, sending him flying backward. He spun through the air, spit flying from his mouth, and landed on his face. But before Daichi could respond with an attack, Kasami summoned another cloud of steam and leapt backward through the mist, shouting, "Try to find me, little fly!"

Ugh, thought Daichi, staring at the wall of steam. *Not this again. Wait a minute… In terms of raw combat, Kasami's strength lies in her martial arts techniques. But when it comes down to her water powers, it seems as if she has only one method of attack. Either that or making steam and ice is the only thing she can do.*

Then Daichi's face lit up in realization.

Wait! That's it! All she's formed with her powers are steam and ice, which means Kasami can only control the temperature of water. Her signature move is trapping her enemies in a cloud of steam, and once she sees movement through the steam, she uses that opportunity to attack quickly and quietly. However, if her enemy remains still and silent, she'll have nothing to target. She'll be forced to make the first move.

With that, Daichi took up an offensive stance and waited in silence.

Outside the steam cloud, Kasami stared at the steam, looking puzzled.

"What the hell's he doing in there?" she muttered. "He better not have pussied out on our fight."

She held out her hand and whispered, "Water freeze."

Once Daichi saw her power activate through the steam, he reached through and grabbed her shoulder.

"Ha!" shouted Daichi. "Gotcha now!"

He retracted his arm and delivered a powerful punch to Kasami's face. She staggered back, staring in disbelief as the steam cleared away.

"I don't believe it," she marveled. "You figured out my power quicker than I expected."

Daichi stepped through the vapors with a determined look on his face.

"Is that all you've got?" he taunted. "Why don't you stop hiding behind your clouds and fight me for real?"

Kasami wiped the blood from her mouth and chuckled.

"Not bad, Daichi. I'm impressed by your versatility. But don't get ahead of yourself, because this time I won't hold back!"

The two of them took up offensive stances, ready to resume their battle.

12 — FIGHT TO THE DEATH

Maddox's heart rate increased with each step. He was rushing with emotions, satisfied he was about to confront his old enemy. Though, remembering what happened to Edmund also awoke the anger inside him, giving him the determination to exact revenge.

He came to halt once he reached the top of the stairs. A faint blue light crept through the cracks of the doorway, as if Mirko's aura was oozing through.

Maddox took a deep breath.

To all the soldiers who lost their lives in the war, all

the victims of the Holocaust, and Edmund, hear me now. Today, your souls will be freed from the monster who stole them from you.

He burst open the door.

Today, you will finally rest in peace.

However, as soon as Maddox stepped foot in the room, he stopped and stared with wide eyes.

"What the?" he muttered.

The penthouse had been altered; all the furniture and plants had been removed, leaving the room empty.

Maddox looked around; Mori wasn't there. Instead, Mirko stood in the center of the room with his arms behind his back, a condescending smirk on his face.

"Congratulations, Maddox," he said. "You've made it to the final stage of the puzzle."

Maddox snorted at his words.

"Shut up," he snapped. "The game's over, Mirko. I've completed all eighty floors, so you keep your promise and release Mori!"

"Oh, I'll keep my promise. However, you have only ascended seventy-nine stories, my friend. By my count, you still have one more to complete. Take a good look at the floor, Maddox. I've arranged these tiles in a specific pattern. Some tiles will hold in place after stepping on them, others may collapse and cause you to fall into the aquarium, which I have also made some modifications to. I've removed all the fish inside and replaced the normal water with heavily oxidized water. So if you happen to slip and fall in, the water will drag you to the bottom in the blink of an eye. Sounds like a fun battleground, doesn't it?"

"For the last time, where are you hiding Mori?"

"Calm down. Didn't I tell you to take a good look at the floor? Like buried treasure, she's right beneath our feet."

Mirko pointed at the tile beneath him.

Maddox looked down. A faint silhouette was visible beneath the glass. He looked closer, and just as Mirko said, Mori was floating inside a bubble, trapped at the bottom of the aquarium. Her body hung there aimlessly, her eyes closed with a blank expression on her face.

"Don't worry," Mirko reassured. "She's not dead. Though, I can't guarantee that she won't be in the next few minutes. You see, I've concealed Mori inside a protective bubble filled with air. Your objective for this floor is to get through me and save her. However, keep in mind that if you use your fire powers, you'll heat the water beneath us. And the hotter the water gets, the more the bubble will shrink. In essence, fighting me will only kill her quicker."

Maddox narrowed his eyes and gritted his teeth.

"I must say, though," Mirko continued, switching to a lighter tone. "I'm impressed you two made it this far. That new Earth Death kid is picking up fast. Speaking of which…"

A menacing smile formed on his face. Then he widened his eyes and spoke intensely, "Did you happen to tell him about how his father died?"

Maddox's eyes widened with rage. Quickly, he summoned flames around his fists and shouted, "Shut up! Yoshito Hara was a greater Death; no, a greater man than you'll ever be! You don't deserve to speak of him!"

He leapt in the air toward Mirko and swung his right fist.

In defense, Mirko raised his hand and shouted, "Water shield!"

Just as Maddox's fist was about to make contact, droplets of water accumulated in the air and formed a body-sized water shield in Mirko's hand.

Maddox punched the shield, pushing Mirko back. Water flew in all directions and a burst of steam emitted from the hole in the shield. Then it formed itself back together.

Maddox clenched his fist, causing the fire to burn brighter, and punched the shield again. This time, he made an even bigger hole. He opened his left hand and conjured a fireball. Then he gripped it with both hands and pressed it against the shield with all his might.

Mirko's hand quivered as he struggled to hold off the flaming sphere. Steam and smoke emanated intensely, until Mirko decided to make the water shield explode. Streams of water splashed everywhere, the force of it sending Mirko and Maddox flying backwards.

Unfortunately for Maddox, when he landed on the floor, his foot fell onto one of the trap tiles and it tipped inwards. In the split second he had to react, he lifted his foot in the air and leapt backwards over the square opening, sliding to a stop.

"Do you want to know, Maddox?" said Mirko, smiling.

"Know what?"

"The gassings; what they were like. Oh, you should have been there. They were like animals, those Jews; dirty, naked, and noisy."

Maddox dashed forward at Mirko, but instead of attacking, he ran past him and slammed his hand on one of the tiles. There was a loud pop and a cloud of smoke burst into the air, surrounding Mirko.

Mirko looked in all directions, but the smoke was too thick to see through. Then all of a sudden, a light, powdery substance hit him in the face, blinding his eyes.

"Nice follow-up with the soot," he complimented, coughing sporadically. "You know something about those Jews, Maddox? It was so much fun listening to them getting gassed. As soon as you dropped in one of those canisters, they banged on the walls like monkeys and screamed like pigs!"

Suddenly, Maddox appeared through the smoke and swung his flaming fist into Mirko's cheek, sending him flying across the room.

Mirko landed on one of the collapsible tiles, which slipped inwards, and he fell into the aquarium.

The oxidized water dragged him to the bottom, flooding his nose and lungs. However, his powers prevented him from drowning. He landed on the floor and stood there, eyeing the bubble containing

Mori.

Hmm, Mirko thought. *It appears the bubble's already decreased in size since the start of our battle. If Maddox keeps this up, it could be the end of Mori.*

Meanwhile up above, water began to splash and spill from the hole where Mirko fell through, the tiles around it cracking. Maddox could feel the glass vibrating beneath his feet. Then the rumbling increased and he dove out of the way.

A surge of water shot from the opening like a geyser with Mirko at the top of the stream. He pointed at Maddox and sent the entire stream flying in his direction.

The stream smashed into Maddox's chest, sending him flying into the wall. Then it gripped him like a giant tentacle and pulled him out of the plaster. It wrapped around his body, preventing his arms and legs from moving.

Mirko landed on the floor and walked up to Maddox, who struggled to free himself from the stream's clutches. Then he raised his hand and the stream lowered Maddox to the floor.

"Now," said Mirko, "allow me to share an example of what I forced upon the Jews; dehydration."

He grabbed Maddox by the neck and activated his powers.

A sharp chill coursed through Maddox's body. Feeling lightheaded, his vision became blurry and his mouth went dry, his veins tightening.

Mirko leaned in closer and chuckled.

"The water in your body's evaporating," he explained, snickering. "In just a few minutes, you'll be nothing but a dried-up bag of bones. Such an embarrassing death, wouldn't you say?"

Maddox's eyes fluttered; he was about to go unconscious. Then suddenly, something under them exploded, knocking Mirko backwards. The stream holding Maddox released itself and splashed onto the floor.

Mirko rose to his feet and grunted in pain. He looked down; his shoes were blackened from the explosion and his leg was bleeding.

"Ach," Mirko grunted, pulling a bloodied shard of glass from his calf. "That stung a little. Just what the hell *was* that, Maddox?"

"One of my fire traps. While you were blinded by my smoke cloud, I placed a bit of my aura into each of the tiles, and I continued to do so after you fell into the aquarium. Every tile is programmed to detonate by my command. So in essence, Mirko, you have nowhere to run."

"Hehe," Mirko simpered. "Not for long. Take a look outside."

Maddox glanced over at the window. Outside, the weather had changed, the skies darkened by storm clouds. A drop of rain struck against the window and streaked downwards, followed by another, then another, until it became a downpour.

Maddox eyed Mirko suspiciously.

"Those storm clouds showed up awfully quick," he remarked. "And I don't recall of any forecasts of rain today. I presume this is the work of one of your

Shinigami?"

"You've cracked the case, Mr. Detective. Indeed, this is the work of my precipitation and condensation Shinigami, Shinji Ono. He's a particularly quiet boy. He isolates himself from the others and barely speaks at all. But don't underestimate him. He is much stronger than he looks."

Outside, standing on the roof of the building closest to the Kanemochi no Hotel was Shinji Ono.

He was a young, eight-year old boy with light brown hair, no taller than four feet, dressed in a gray zip-up jacket and jeans. He stood there motionless as he stared into the sky, the raindrops hitting softly against his cheeks, the storm clouds circling the top of the hotel.

Inside the hotel, Mirko smiled and continued, "Thanks to him, he's given me an infinite supply of my element."

He raised his hands at Maddox and a swarm of raindrops from outside smashed through the windows like bullets, shattering glass everywhere. As they whizzed through the air toward Maddox, they formed into thin needles.

Maddox conjured another cloud of smoke, concealing himself. Then the water-needles flew into the smoke and disappeared from sight.

Mirko couldn't tell whether the needles made contact or not until suddenly, Maddox came flying through the smoke, propelling himself by shooting flames from his hands and feet like rockets.

Maddox grabbed Mirko by the collar and flew out the window. As they soared through the rainstorm, he pummeled Mirko in the face repeatedly. Then he grabbed his shirt and hurtled him into the side of a nearby building. Concrete smashed everywhere, leaving a man-shaped hole in the wall with Mirko inside.

Maddox raced over to the building and yanked Mirko out of the wall. He pulled him close, eyeing him angrily, and dropped him.

Maddox crossed his arms and watched, levitating stationary in the air as Mirko became a speck, plummeting hundreds of feet into the streets below.

Maddox spat and glided back toward the hotel. Then suddenly, something grabbed him by his jacket and pulled him upwards.

It was Mirko, and he was propelling himself through the air by emitting a cloud of steam beneath him, using it as a lifting gas.

He carried Maddox further and further up, until they were so high, the hotel was lost from view. Then he hurtled Maddox's body into the air.

Rain and wind pounded against Maddox's face as he raced into the sky, soaring above the clouds.

Meanwhile, Mirko extended his arms and formed the rainwater into a giant serpent-like stream. As Maddox descended, Mirko thrust his arms forward and the stream shot through the air like an anaconda, snatching up Maddox.

The stream hurtled him into multiple buildings,

moving at an intense speed. Concrete and glass exploded everywhere, whilst Mirko levitated in the midst of it all, smirking maliciously.

Enjoying himself, he raised his hands and summoned four more streams. Moving rapidly, they slithered through the air and struck Maddox repeatedly, flinging him like a rag doll.

The first stream slammed into his face and blood flew from his mouth. The second stream followed up from below by crashing against his spine. Then the third swung itself like a hammer and pounded Maddox in the stomach, hurling him into the fourth which swung its 'tail' and battered his legs.

Mirko meshed his hands and the four streams merged together, forming one massive stream the size of a freight train. Then, with the wave of Mirko's hand, the stream charged at Maddox and plowed him through the wall of one of the skyscrapers, blasting him out the other end.

Maddox was beaten. His body was so bruised, he could barely move. He drifted in and out of consciousness as he plummeted to the ground, his eyes fluttering. Then everything turned dark and the pounding of the raindrops faded.

Maddox jolted awake, feeling a sudden rush of energy. He was lying on the floor, back in the penthouse. He turned his head; Mirko was kneeling next to him, holding an injected syringe in Maddox's arm.

Maddox jumped to his feet and removed the syringe.

"That was an adrenaline shot, wasn't it?" he said immediately.

Mirko snickered.

"Why?!" Maddox shouted.

He threw the syringe across the room.

"Why didn't you just kill me while I was out?"

"Come now. That wouldn't have been a satisfying death, Maddox; neither for you nor me. I want to see you suffer to the very end."

Maddox narrowed his eyes.

"Haven't you had enough fun?" he growled. "After all the lives you've taken?"

He took up an offensive stance and ignited his flaming fists.

"You've lived long enough."

Mirko summoned a water ball around each hand.

"Maybe we both have," he muttered.

With that, Maddox and Mirko darted at each other, fully prepared to attack, and fully prepared to die.

13 — GRAVITY BREAK

On the seventy-ninth floor, Daichi and Kasami stood in position to attack. However, Daichi began to feel doubts as he took up his stance.

Kasami smirked; she could see the uncertainty in Daichi's face. Taking advantage of his trepidation, she sprinted forward and leapt into the air, then delivered a flying right kick to Daichi's jaw. She followed up with a palm strike to Daichi's chest which sent him flying through the air. He smashed through one of the doors, breaking it in two, and collided with the wall of the hotel room. Then he slumped down and bumped into the dresser next to him, knocking several pieces of china onto the floor, along with a bowl of apples which spilled all over his head.

Ugh, Daichi thought, sitting himself up. *My body feels so heavy.*

The last apple rolled off the dresser and plopped on Daichi's head, falling into his lap.

"Stupid apple," he grunted, picking it up.

He rubbed his head and stared at the fruit, deep in thought.

The main force of Earth that moves and accelerates objects is gravity. Does this mean that all those times where I moved the stone in the walls or caused earthquakes, I was manipulating gravity? That must be it! If the central force of the Earth is gravity, then that must be the central force of my power!

His thoughts were interrupted when Kasami kicked down the wreckage of the door and walked in. She stopped in front of Daichi and hoisted him up by his shirt.

"Come on," she spat. "Are you just going to sit on your ass all day?"

She heaved his body with all her might and sent him smashing through the wall again. Then she stepped through the doorway and stood there, chuckling at the sight of Daichi's limp body in the hallway.

"Pathetic," she scoffed. "You might as well quit if this is how you plan to defend yourself."

Then Daichi did something unusual. He pushed

himself back up, but instead of making a stance, he knelt on the floor with one knee and lowered his head, closing his eyes.

Kasami raised an eyebrow and tilted her head to the side, staring in confusion.

"Earth powers," boomed Daichi. "All gravity levels in this room…"

He raised his hand and activated his aura.

"BREAK!"

Daichi slammed his hand onto the floor and the aura crackled and sparked, shooting down his arm like a surge of electricity. Then there was a loud bang. For a moment, the room remained still. Then all of a sudden, sections of the floor broke off and shot upward, stopping short in midair and levitating, as if floating in space.

Even Kasami rose up and hovered amongst the debris, her black hair fluttering about.

"What the hell?" she muttered, staring at Daichi with wide eyes.

Kneeling with his head down, Daichi spoke.

"Center of gravity…"

He lifted his head and looked Kasami in the eye.

"Direct on Kasami Usui!"

The room shook violently. Rubble crumbled from the ceiling and parts of the wall began to crack. Then, all the debris raced toward Kasami. Large chunks of wall broke off and shot in her direction, followed by sections of ceiling from above.

Kasami had nowhere to run. All she could do was watch as the wreckage hurtled her way.

Then the debris smashed into her. The larger portions concealed her, while the smaller portions massed around the outside, giving the appearance of a large boulder.

Daichi lifted his hand and deactivated his power. The gravity levels returned to normal and the mass of debris released itself, crashing onto the floor.

Daichi stared in amazement at the mountain of rubble.

"I-I did it!" he sputtered. "I can't believe that actually worked!"

He ran up to the wreckage and laughed victoriously.

"Ha! How does it feel to lose, Kasami? Bet you didn't see that one coming, you bitch!"

He kicked a chunk of stone and started away. Then he heard a muffled yell from under the rubble.

Daichi whipped around. Then suddenly, he was knocked backwards. Something exploded from under the rubble, causing the debris to fly everywhere, damaging the room even further. Some of the rubble hit Daichi, sending him flying back.

The smoke cleared to reveal Kasami, who stood with her fists clenched, emitting wisps of steam.

She glared at Daichi, her face brooding with murderous intent, and spoke, "I'll admit that was impressive, but if you thought an attack like that could kill me, you're a fool."

"But… how?!"

"Simple; I used my power to superheat the water in the air, resulting in a massive steam explosion."

Daichi inched back nervously.

"You know, kid," she continued, "I haven't taken you seriously at all this entire fight. But now you've proven yourself. I'm done going easy."

Kasami summoned a cloud of steam and concealed herself. Then the cloud condensed and raced along the floor toward Daichi. Once the steam reached his feet, Kasami burst out and delivered an upward kick to Daichi's stomach.

Daichi grunted in pain and coughed up blood. Her attack felt far more painful than before.

Well, Daichi thought. *I guess this is it.*

Kasami followed up by ramming her fist into Daichi's cheek.

I'm really going to die.

Kasami pummeled his chest with a combo of palm strikes, followed by a butterfly kick to the face.

No, this can't be it. Not now. I still have to save Mori!

Daichi tried desperately to land a punch, but Kasami blocked it without difficulty. Then she replied with a low roundhouse kick to Daichi's legs, a middle one to his chest, and a high one to his face which sent him flying backwards. He landed on his back and sat up.

Slowly, Kasami approached him.

Who am I kidding? How can I save Mori if I can't even save myself?

Kasami opened her hand and formed an ice sword. Daichi scrambled back, but it was clear there was no escape. She lifted the sword over her head and swung downward. Daichi shielded with his hand and scrambled back further. Then there was a flash of blood.

I should just face it; I'm weak. I always have been. My whole life, I've had to rely on others to protect me.

Daichi didn't feel any pain at first. Not until he saw his left hand flying through the air, spurting a trail of blood like a sprinkler.

He jumped to his feet and covered the end of his wounded arm with his right hand to prevent any further blood loss. Kasami lifted the bloody ice sword and swung several more times. Rushing with adrenaline, Daichi dodged each of her incoming swings, and as he did so, his life flashed before his eyes.

He remembered back to a day when he was little, when a group of boys tried beating him up back in grade school. It happened in the playground outside the elementary school when he angered a group of three boys known as the Taniguchi Brothers when he chimed in on their conversation.

Tetsuo Taniguchi, the tallest of the three, grabbed Daichi by his shirt and shoved him to the ground.

"Shut your mouth!" he shouted, glowering at him. "You're such a pest!"

"Yeah!" yelled Toshio Taniguchi, the shortest of the three. "What do you know about teaching?"

"Who cares?!" Daichi retorted. "I told you what I think. Mrs. Takashina is a stupid teacher! That's right, stupid!"

The Taniguchis gasped at his words.

"You heard me! She's too bossy and she gives way too much homework!"

Tsuneo Taniguchi, the second tallest brother, scowled at Daichi and stalked toward him, cracking his knuckles.

"You take that back!" he bellowed. "Or else we're going to tell Mrs. Takashina what you said. But first, brothers, let's teach him a lesson of our own."

Tsuneo retracted his fist, preparing a punch. Daichi scrambled back along the grass and shielded with his hand. He knew there was no way he could win against them. At that moment, all seemed hopeless, until a familiar voice from behind him shouted, "Leave him alone!"

It was Mori.

She ran up to them, moving as fast as she could, and stopped in front of Daichi, shielding him from the Taniguchis.

She stood with her arms outstretched, preventing Tsuneo from getting any closer. She narrowed her eyes and sneered intimidatingly. Toshio and Tsuneo nodded to each other and backed away. However, Tetsuo held his ground and remained firm, scowling at the girl.

"Mori…" Daichi muttered in astonishment.

Mori turned to look at Daichi and smiled.

"Don't worry, Daichi," she whispered, winking at him. "I'll protect you from those meanies."

Daichi never forgot that day. Ever since they were children, Mori always chose to stay by Daichi's side; no matter what.

His memories flashed to another time during his childhood when he, Mori, and Tsubaki went to go play a game of tag at an open field, and they bickered over teams.

"I want Mori on my team," Daichi pouted.

"Stop it, Daichi," said Tsubaki. "Mori's on my team and that's final."

"No, Tsubaki," said Mori suddenly.

She walked over to Daichi and hugged his arm playfully.

"I should be on Daichi's team. Besides, you run fast. It wouldn't be fair to leave Daichi all by himself."

"Fine," Tsubaki grumbled, his cheeks flushing.

Once again, Mori stood by his side. She never left him out, even for the littlest things.

Daichi never truly realized this until a few months ago, when their high school held its annual 'Parent's Day'.

Of course, Daichi never looked forward to Parent's day. While the students explored the hallways with their parents, introducing them to their teachers, Daichi sat on a bench by the main entrance, alone.

He stared sourly at the Parent's Day flyer in his hands. Agitated by the whole situation, he crumpled the paper and tossed it aside.

"What does it matter?" he muttered. "They're both gone anyway."

He looked up and noticed Mori and her father standing nearby with Tsubaki and his father. But he didn't want to get up and join them; he was too ill-tempered to do so.

Tsubaki's father was a tall man in his fifties,

dressed in a sharp business suit. He had wavy, combed-over black hair, and a mustache and chin beard. He shook hands with Chief Mori, smiling with sharp, firm eyes.

"It's nice to see you again, Dr. Tsubaki," said Chief Mori.

"Likewise," said Dr. Tsubaki in a dignified manner.

Tsubaki stood behind his father with his hands in his pockets, looking away uncomfortably. Mori noticed this and frowned. Just by his expression, it was clear Tsubaki suffered a lot of pressure and discipline from his father.

Well, thought Daichi, *at least that's something I'll never have to worry about.*

He stared ahead and sighed, a tear welling in his eye.

Though, it would be nice to have someone like that; someone who cares about your future, who helps you move forward in life. I guess that's something I'll never have.

Daichi's thoughts were interrupted when he glanced to the side; Mori was sitting next to him on the bench. She stared at him with a sincere look in her eyes, as if she could tell what was going through his head. Gently, she took his hand and smiled.

Daichi blushed and gazed at her, at a loss for words.

Mori giggled and eased closer to him on the bench.

"You didn't think I'd leave you all alone now, did you?"

It was at that moment when Daichi realized how much Mori cared for him. And now, as Daichi continued to dodge the swings of Kasami's ice sword, he felt like he had never truly repaid her.

Daichi ducked and avoided another one of Kasami's slashes, but when he stood up, his back hit against something hard. He looked behind, and to his horror, he was standing against the elevator doors.

Kasami snickered nastily. She had him cornered. There was no way for him to escape.

Daichi stood there in shock, petrified against the elevator. He couldn't move a muscle; he was too scared to do so.

Kasami retracted the hilt and her face turned serious. Then she thrust the sword forward.

Daichi jerked his head and let out a sharp, piercing grunt. Then he looked down; a chill ran down his spine at the sight of the blade protruding from his stomach.

At that moment, a stream of memories flowed through Daichi's brain like photos in a slideshow.

Not once, Daichi thought. *All my friends, my family, they've always protected me, but not once have I protected them.*

Faces of the people he knew flashed through his head; Mori, Haruka, Tsubaki, Chief Mori, Maddox, his mother, and just as he was about to see his father, he was pulled back to reality when Kasami yanked the sword from his stomach, causing a stream of blood to gush onto the floor.

Daichi couldn't breathe. He became light-headed, and everything in sight went fuzzy. Then he lost all feeling in his legs and he slumped to the floor, leaving a streak of blood down the elevator doors.

His mind wavered. In his dying breath, Daichi reached out his hand and sputtered, "No... I have... to save her."

He let out one last cough. Then his eyes shut and his body became still. His hand fell limply to the floor and his head slumped into his lap.

"Pathetic," snorted Kasami as she stared upon the dismal sight of her enemy's body. "I expected more out of you, Daichi Hara."

She lowered her sword and heated it with her powers, melting it into water. After it spilled from her hands and onto the floor, she turned around and walked toward the end of the hallway.

Then she stopped and spoke, "Though, I'll admit, you put up a pretty good fight for a-"

But when Kasami turned around to take on last look at Daichi, she stopped speaking.

Daichi was on his feet, with an intense aura surrounding him. However, this aura was of a totally different nature compared to his Death aura. Its color or was a morphed combination of white and black, and it swirled around him like a tornado, causing his hair to wave about. His entire body appeared white; even his eyes.

Kasami was petrified by the sight of it; but what frightened her most was the expression on Daichi's face. He stared at her, calm and composed, with a serious glare in the white pupils of his eyes, not showing the slightest sign of pain despite the fatal wounds he received.

Kasami had no idea of what to make of it. It was unlike anything she had ever seen.

14 - ???

Kasami gaped with wide eyes at the newly en-
hanced Daichi, not sure whether to attack or not. But
then she remembered Mirko's orders, and imagined
how he would react if she told him Daichi beat her.

Cautiously, she readied her hand to form another ice weapon. However, the moment she made a
move, Daichi spoke.

"Don't."

The power amplified his voice, making him sound
more mature and sophisticated.

Kasami couldn't believe what she was hearing. It was as if he were a completely different person. Dismissing his command, she formed an ice spear and charged.

Daichi did not move from where he stood. His face didn't show the slightest trace of fear, not even as she drove the spear through his heart.

Kasami expected Daichi react in some shape or form, but all he did was stand there, as if nothing happened.

He looked down at the spear and raised his eyebrows. Then he looked up and smirked.

Kasami widened her eyes in shock.

Then Daichi opened his right hand and a black orb formed in his palm, its energy swirling like the clouds of a gas giant. When he placed it against the spear, the ice disintegrated into particles, and the orb sucked them into its void like a black hole.

Kasami gasped and backed away, but Daichi wasn't finished.

He closed his hand, making the orb disappear, and opened it again. A white orb appeared in his palm.

He placed the orb against the wound in his heart and it shrunk itself, glowing intensely. A moment later, the brightness stabilized and it returned to its original size. When Daichi removed the orb, his chest was unscathed.

He placed the orb over his belly and healed the wound in his stomach. Then he placed it over the bloody stub of his left arm. When he removed it, his left hand was back in place, clean and uninjured.

Daichi closed his hand and extinguished the orb.

There was a long silence. Then Daichi closed his eyes and suddenly, it felt as though time stopped. The energy of his aura grew in intensity, leaving Kasami frozen in fear. He lifted his foot and took a step toward Kasami. The time it took for his foot to land seemed like an eternity. Then Kasami blinked, and when she opened her eyes, Daichi was standing in front of her, his face just inches from hers.

Kasami gasped and jolted backward.

Daichi closed his eyes and took a deep breath. As he inhaled, his aura compressed itself, consuming all the light in the room. Then he opened his eyes and exhaled, causing his aura to erupt, emitting waves of energy as strong as the winds of a hurricane.

Kasami was knocked off her feet and blown backward into the wall. She struggled to free herself, but the energy was too strong. The wall behind her began to crack. Then it gave way and she crashed through. Her body hurtled across the bedroom and smashed through the window, shattering glass everywhere as she plummeted to the ground.

Daichi inhaled again and his aura stabilized.

The hallway was quiet now. Daichi stood there motionless, as if waiting for something.

A moment later, there was a violent shake from above and he looked up. The lights on the ceiling flickered.

He narrowed his eyes and frowned, as if he could see what was happening. Then Daichi turned and walked to the end of the hallway. Once he reached the staircase, his aura spiked, a grim look ridding his face. Then he lifted his foot and stepped onto the first stair. A burst of energy emitted from his aura.

Slowly, he ascended the stairs.

Mirko was the first to attack. He summoned a gush of water and shot it at Maddox's mouth, planning to send it down his windpipe. However, just before the stream met his lips, Maddox opened his hands and a heat wave burst from his aura, evaporating the water instantly.

Mirko followed up by summoning five masses of water which he then formed into grunts.

Once they were fully shaped, the grunts darted at him all at once. The first grunt snuck up behind Maddox and locked his arms, while the other four surrounded him in a circle. The second grunt pummeled him in the face repeatedly. Then the grunt restraining Maddox released him and the third grunt karate chopped his upper torso. Then Maddox stumbled back into the fourth grunt, who delivered three front kicks, followed by a butterfly kick to the face which knocked him to the floor.

Before he could even attempt to get up, the fifth grunt stooped over Maddox and raised its hands. Its watery fingers manifested into sharp claws. Then, like an animal, it moved in and slashed rapidly at his face.

There was a flash of blood and Maddox let out a cry of pain.

As the grunts' brutal assaults progressed, Mirko

168

folded his arms and snickered.

Daichi's aura swirled faster. His clothes fluttered and his hair waved wildly, as if he were walking through a storm.

He took another step. When his foot landed, the wood of the stair broke in half, as if his feet were made of lead.

The light shining through the edges of the door-way became brighter, and as he neared the top, so did the glimmer in his white eyes.

Another punch, another kick, followed by several more slashes; the grunts made sure not to give Maddox the slightest opportunity to defend.

Maddox's face was injured so badly, he looked deformed. There were purple bruises everywhere, along with several gashes in his forehead and cheeks. His nose was broken, his lips were swollen and discolored, and he could barely see out of his eyes.

Mirko raised his hand.

"Enough," he ordered.

The grunts halted their attacks and stared at their master.

Maddox stumbled about and fell to his knees, lowering his head in defeat.

Mirko waved his hand and the grunts dispersed into a puddle of water. Then he took a step toward Maddox. However, when he did, Maddox lifted his head and formed a finger gun with his hand.

He pulled his middle finger like a trigger and shot a small flame from his pointer finger.

The flame was compressed into the shape of a bullet. However, just as it was about to pierce through Mirko's skull, a water shield appeared in front of his face and it extinguished the bullet.

Mirko slid his hands into his pockets and smirked.

Maddox fired two more times, but once again, Mirko countered them, summoning one shield over his heart and one over his stomach.

Amidst his anger and desperation, Maddox sprayed a series of flame bullets in rapid succession.

But it was to no avail. Water shields popped up in front of Mirko no matter where Maddox shot. Slowly, he walked up to Maddox, who continued to fire.

Maddox's finger was just inches from Mirko's heart, and he was firing at the rate of a machine gun.

Mirko looked down on Maddox disappointedly and snatched his hand, gripping it tightly.

"Come now," he said, sounding annoyed. "Is that *really* the best you can do? What did those Americans teach you in the military, how to shove a pistol up your ass?"

With an intense amount of force, Mirko yanked Maddox's arm straight out and slammed his hand into his elbow. There was a loud crack and Maddox grunted in pain.

Immediately following up, Mirko kneed Maddox in the chest and sent him flying into the wall.

Maddox crashed so hard it broke some of the plaster behind him. He slumped down the wall and sat there, looking defeated as Mirko stalked toward him. He couldn't feel anything in his right arm any longer, and his face was in searing pain, as well as his chest; several of his ribs had been broken. As for his legs, they were so weak he couldn't bring himself to stand.

All he could do was sit there and wait for his enemy finish him.

Mirko grabbed Maddox by his tattered shirt and hoisted him up.

"I expected more of a fight out of you, Maddox. Yet here you are, without the strength to lift so much as a finger against me. How embarrassing."

Daichi was a few steps away from the top.

His aura glowed so bright, the entire stairwell appeared white.

He stopped at the top of the stairs and reached for the doorknob, his aura spiraling around his body like a tornado. As his hand closed in, the wood of the door vibrated and creaked, shooting splinters like bullets.

Mirko waved his hand three times. Three streams of water summoned from his palm and flew at Maddox. One spun around his right arm, another around his left arm, and another around his neck, circling in a donut shape.

"You couldn't even manage to save Mizuki," he said bitterly, scowling at Maddox. "Yoshito and Edmund would be disappointed."

Mirko snapped his fingers and the streams increased in speed and compressed in shape, becoming thin as paper and sharp as blades. Slowly, they neared Maddox's skin.

However, the attack was interrupted when Daichi grabbed the doorknob.

The door exploded from the touch of his aura, as if a miniature bomb went off. Wood chippings and shards of metal flew everywhere.

Mirko whipped around and the water blades dispersed, splashing to the ground just as they were about to slice Maddox. Then Mirko released him.

Maddox fell to the floor and rolled to his side. He opened his eyes as best as he could to see who was there. Everything in sight was blurry, though he could see a faint silhouette through the smoke.

Mirko could see it too. Gradually, the smoke cleared to reveal Daichi. He stalked broodingly toward Mirko with his hands clenched.

Maddox gasped at the sight of Daichi with his unusual aura.

Mirko narrowed his eyes and frowned.

So, he thought, *that Earth Death kid made it past Kasami; impressive. But something doesn't feel right. When I first saw him, he was nothing but a loud mouthed brat; full of fear and uncertainty. But… that look in his eyes; I don't sense any fear. It's as if he genuinely believes he can kill me. And what's going on with his aura? Back when Yoshito was the Earth Death, his aura was always green. I don't ever recall him conjuring this sort of energy. Something about it feels off. Just standing next to it, I*

172

feel like there's something surrounding me, like I'm being constricted. And by the look on Maddox's face, it's clear he's never seen it before either.

Daichi stopped before Mirko and stood there, eyeing him silently. Then he looked down at the floor and his face turned somber at the sight of the bubble containing Mori. He lifted his head, and when his eyes met with Mirko's, he scowled grievously.

Mirko stared at the boy silently, both baffled and curious by his demeanor.

Daichi took one more step; then he hawked noisily and spat on Mirko's shoe.

Mirko gaped at the boy for a moment; then he looked down at the gob of wet, bubbling saliva that sullied his left leather shoe.

He looked up at Daichi and frowned. Then suddenly, he burst out laughing, cackling maniacally as if someone told him the funniest joke in the world. He sighed and wiped a tear from his eye.

"Never," he said, his laughter slowing.

"Never," he said again, this time more serious.

"NEVER," he shouted, his face wild like a madman.

Daichi's face remained firm

Mirko panted heavily then continued, "Never in my years as a Death have I met ANYONE with anywhere NEAR as much gall as you! You know, I was toying with the idea of letting you live for a bit so I could fight you. But now, you've lost that opportunity."

Mirko opened his palm and activated his aura.

Then he reached onto his palm with his other hand and pulled out a long thread of water. He released the strand and let it float in the air, wriggling as if it were alive.

"You see this?" said Mirko, indicating the squirming strand of water. "This is one of my water tapeworms; twice as deadly as a normal tapeworm, and replicates by the minute. If one of these enters your body, it'll eat you alive from the inside. A most excruciating death; it's not a technique I use often. Only when I want to take pleasure in watching my enemies suffer do I use it."

The entire time Mirko spoke, Daichi's expression remained unchanged. He didn't even glance at the wriggling tapeworm. His eyes were fixed on Mirko.

Daichi's static demeanor made Mirko feel uneasy. The tapeworm technique instilled fear in the hearts of even his most courageous enemies. But Daichi didn't even acknowledge it.

Mirko scowled angrily and shouted, "You think I'm joking around?! Very well, see for yourself!"

Mirko retracted his arm and threw his hand forward, sending the water tapeworm slithering through the air, headed straight for Daichi's mouth. However, just as it was about to make contact with his lips, Daichi made a swift motion with his arm and caught the tapeworm with two fingers.

Mirko gasped in shock. This was the first time someone successfully countered his tapeworm attack.

But Daichi wasn't finished. He lifted the tapeworm to his mouth and swallowed it whole. Then he opened his hand and summoned the black orb in his palm. He opened his mouth and a stream of tiny particles fluttered from the back of his throat, drifting through the air and into the orb. Once all the particles were consumed, Daichi closed his hand and the orb disappeared.

Mirko backed away and shuddered.

"What is this power?" he muttered.

Determined to defeat Daichi, Mirko raised his hands and summoned a water ball large enough to contain a human; then he pushed forward, sending it hurtling at Daichi.

Daichi let the water ball surround him, not even attempting to dodge it. Then he placed his hands together and summoned the black orb between them. It spun rapidly, rippling the surface of the water ball. Then gradually, the water ball shrunk down, and it was gone; devoured by the black orb.

Mirko scrunched his face in anger, looking like a serial killer. In his frustration, he gave a battle cry and flailed his hands. Numerous streams of water appeared in the air and shot toward Daichi, moving at incredible speeds.

Reacting calmly, Daichi placed the black orb in the palm of his hand and approached Mirko. The orb spun rapidly and sucked in the streams like a vacuum, regardless of how fast they were going. Once all the streams were gone, Daichi stopped in front of Mirko and glared at him.

Mirko dropped his hands and panted, staring furiously into Daichi's white eyes.

As they glared at each other in silence, a smile formed on Daichi's face. Then he raised an eyebrow and said, "Is that it?"

"Why?!" Mirko shouted. "Why do you live?!"

Daichi remained silent. Then he retracted his arm and opened his hand. A black and white morphed orb appeared in his palm.

"Because I can," he replied.

With tremendous force, Daichi thrust his hand forward and up, smashing the orb into Mirko's stomach. Mirko grunted and spit flew from his mouth. The force of the collision lifted him off the ground, knocking the air out of him.

The orb sparked and made a whirring sound, glowing brighter than ever.

Mirko felt a rush of energy channeling throughout his body.

What is this? Is this power going to kill me? Nein, *it can't be! I will not lose to someone as unexperienced as him!*

Daichi removed his hand and Mirko's body returned to normal.

"What the hell was that?!" Mirko bellowed, fumbling his hands over his stomach. "What did you do to me?"

Daichi stepped back and snickered.

"ANSWER ME!"

Mirko snapped his fingers and two grunts appeared behind Daichi. They charged forward and hurled their fists at him.

Daichi whipped around and summoned the white orb in his hand. Then, with his free hand, he reached inside it and pulled out a glowing white energy sword.

He leapt forward and sliced through the torsos of both grunts. The sword made a loud bang when it made contact. Then the grunts decomposed, breaking down into a disarray of particles.

Daichi landed on the floor and extinguished the energy sword. Then he opened his right hand and summoned the black orb.

As the particles flowed into the orb, Maddox stared at Daichi in bewilderment from where he lay.

A look of frustration filled Mirko's eyes. Clenching his fists, he roared at the top of his lungs and rushed at Daichi, activating his aura. He summoned a mass of water in the air which hovered and rippled. Then he waved his hands and the water shot a multitude of streams at Daichi.

Daichi dodged the attacks effortlessly.

Such precise movements, Mirko thought. *Such gracefulness in his steps. It appears as if I'm going easy on him, but I'm not. I'm attacking him with my full strength. Hell, I'm probably using more of my power on him than I used on Maddox!*

Mirko waved his hand and evaporated the water streams; then he formed a water ball around each fist. He ran up to Daichi and punched at him repeatedly. However, to his dismay, Daichi blocked each blow with ease.

The water balls feel heavier than usual. Nein, *I'm fool-*

ing myself. I must be losing confidence in my ability to win. I feel… weak. Ever since I was made a Death, I aspired to become the most powerful of the four, and after World War II, I felt like I had finally achieved that goal. But now, for once since then, I don't feel in control. Part of me envies his abilities. But there's no denying; this kid's handling my attacks stupendously. Not once have I landed a successful hit on him. Back when I was an ordinary human, I met some tough fighters. Though, they all had one thing in common. They were sloppy; driven solely by their anger, not from concentration and technique. But this kid's so composed when he blocks. I can feel it in his arms. Normally, you feel a rushing, nervous tension when you make contact with your opponent's body during a fight. But with him, I don't feel anything. His resolve can only compare to the most archaic of fighters.

Mirko leapt back and extended his arms, summoning six water rings in the air. They flew toward Daichi and stacked themselves downwards, surrounding him. Then they formed together and circled rapidly, creating a vortex which Daichi trapped inside.

Hold on. That vortex took far too long to summon, and the rings are supposed to spin faster than that.

The vortex shifted inward, distorting wildly. Then the water disappeared, only to reveal Daichi holding the black orb.

Mirko looked Daichi in the eye and said, "That black and white orb did something to me, didn't it? My powers feels sluggish, like something inside me is weighing me down. It's no secret, so why don't you speak to me like a man and stop being a *verdammt wenig scheisskopf*?"

Daichi extinguished the orb with his hand and his face turned serious.

"You really want to know?" he said.

"Enough screwing around, you little wretch!" snapped Mirko through gritted teeth.

"You said you feel something in your body?" Daichi asked enigmatically. "The connection's being severed, Fleischer."

Mirko narrowed his eyes in confusion, not sure what to say.

"What's that supposed to mean?" he asked, fed up with his mysteriousness.

"Can't you see?" rang Maddox's voice.

Mirko whipped around. Maddox was pushing himself up.

He pressed his hand against his back and straightened his knees, grunting along the way. When he made it to his feet, he opened his bruised eyelids and muttered, "Well Mirko? Can't you see how far you've fallen?"

Mirko snorted at his words.

"Enough out of you! Can't you see I'm trying to get an answer out of this little *arschloch* right now?!"

"Daichi; his name is Daichi. Haven't you figured it out yet, Mirko? He's already told you. The connection's being severed, meaning the connection between your body and your Death item. By my guess, it was caused by that black and white orb he struck you in the chest with. I'm not sure what it does, but it looks like the orb transferred its energy to you, and now it's channeling through your body, emitting waves that act as a repellant to your Death powers. Basically Mirko, you're going to lose control of your powers."

Mirko's eyes shifted from Maddox to Daichi nervously, drops of sweat streaking down his forehead. He looked down at his hands and gulped, the side of his lips quivering.

Is this it? Is this the sensation I feel in my body; what's weighing me down? An energy that is eradicating the gift that inspired me from the start; the blessing that has protected me no matter who or what stood in my way; the force that has sustained my life all these years? Nein... I can't simply bid them farewell. I need them to move further. Why... why does it have to be this way? I cherish my powers. They support me. They encourage me. They care for me, as I care for them. If it weren't for them, I never would've made it this far.

A drop of water suddenly appeared in the palm of Mirko's hand. However, he was confused. He hadn't activated his aura, so he had no idea how he summoned it. Only when he lifted his hand to his face did Mirko realize it wasn't just a drop of water; it was a tear.

There was a tense silence, until finally, Mirko lifted his head and spoke.

"How long?" he asked sullenly. "How long will this effect last on me?"

Daichi stared at him with a blank expression. Then his lips formed into a smirk.

"Who knows?"

15 — FORGE MY OWN PATH

Throughout the day, Chief Mori was agitated, unnerved by the situation. He stayed at home the rest of the day in order to relax, but whenever he tried doing so, the thought of his daughter kidnapped kept popping back up in his head.

After Maddox left, he drank a cup of tea then went back to bed. However, his slumber was interrupted by a nightmare he had; a nightmare in which he imagined himself confronting the kidnapper, but as soon as he moved in to capture him, the kidnapper raised his hand. That's when Chief Mori stopped running. There, held by the hair, was his daughter's severed head.

Chief Mori burst awake and panted heavily, sweat dripping down his face.

He took a shower afterwards. Once he was dried and dressed, Chief Mori sat down on the couch in his living room. He looked over at the picture sitting on the table next to him and smiled.

It was a picture of his late wife cradling an infant girl in her arms.

He picked up the picture and gazed at her smiling face, a glint in his eyes.

She was a beautiful woman in her mid-thirties at the time of the photo. She had long brown hair and brown eyes, and she wore a red collared shirt with a dark red gardening apron overtop. In her arms, a young infant girl stared into the camera with a huge smile, happy to be with her mother.

"Suzume," said Chief Mori. "I'm sure you're more at peace right now than I am."

His smile turned into a somber frown and a tear formed in his eye. He sniffed and wiped away the tear with his sleeve.

"I'm sorry, Suzume," he muttered, trying to hold back any further tears. "I'm sorry I let this happen. I'm sorry I wasn't there to save her. I wish you were here to see how much our daughter's grown. She's kind, beautiful, and intelligent. So much like you, Suzume."

Chief Mori rested his face in his hand and sobbed

quietly, until he was interrupted by the ringing of his cell phone.

He placed down the picture and pulled himself together; then he answered the phone.

"Hello?"

"Hello Chief. It's Officer Hayashi. Have you seen the reports on television yet?"

"What?"

"Turn on your TV."

Chief Mori grabbed the remote and clicked on the television.

A weather woman was giving a report on an unexpected thunderstorm that's made its way over the Tokyo metropolitan area. Then it forwarded to a breaking news report of the Shinjuku district, showing a helicopter view of a human shaped crater on the side of a building. Then it cut to a wide view of the buildings, showing sections of shattered glass windows.

Chief Mori's eyes widened when he saw the Kanemochi no Hotel amongst the damaged buildings. He sat up in his chair and spoke into the phone.

"Hayashi, I want all available units to assemble outside the Kanemochi no Hotel now. And call in the Special Assault Team. No one makes a move till I get there."

"Alright, sir. See you there."

Chief Mori hung up the phone and rose to his feet. He took one last look at the picture and put on his hat.

I can't trust Maddox with this case any longer. Besides,

I should be the one saving her.

With that, Chief Mori threw on his trench coat and headed out the door.

Atop the office building next to the Kanemochi no Hotel, Shinji stared into the sky, manipulating the nimbus clouds precipitating above. Despite his clothes were drenched and the winds were frigid, he showed no emotion or feeling whatsoever. It seemed as if he didn't have a care for anything aside from his mission.

Suddenly, he was interrupted when two janitors came rushing up through the roof door.

The first man stepped forward, his jacket waving like a flag in the wind, and shouted, "Hey kid! What the hell are you doing up here?! It's too dangerous!"

Shinji made no reaction to the sound of their voices.

"Why don't you come with us?" the other man spoke.

Shinji whipped his head around like a doll and stared into their eyes. His blank expression remained unchanged.

Both men shuddered beneath their coats

There was a long silence.

"Um, kid?" the first man spoke.

All of a sudden, the first man felt a moist sensation in his lungs building up rapidly. He began to cough, turning into a violent fit, then he stooped over and hurled a large gush of water.

The second man put his hand on his shoulder and

asked, "Hey man, you okay?"

The first man straightened himself and tilted his head back with his mouth open. He grabbed his neck and made a gurgling, choking sound. Water spilled from his eyelids, ears, and nose. Then he fell, landing on his backside, and made one last gurgle.

The second man stared frozen in horror at the gruesome sight of his friend's dead body.

His eyes darted to Shinji, but when they did, a searing pain coursed through the veins in his arms, bulging like they were swelling up. The man clutched his arms and dropped to his knees, howling in pain. All the veins in his body bulged outward like an array of electrical wires. Then they popped all at once, spattering blood across the rooftop.

Shinji turned back around as if nothing happened; then he walked to the edge of the rooftop and looked down. Far below, he could see the red and blue lights of police cars gathering in the street below, in front of the Kanemochi no Hotel.

Shinji sighed through his nose and walked back to the center of the rooftop, the police being of no concern to him.

Down below, a mass of police cars were parked outside the hotel. There were so many officers, it looked like an army. Some were busy creating detours at the ends of the street to keep civilians away, while the rest loaded their weapons and strapped on bullet proof vests. At the entrance stood the TPD Special Assault Team, or the 'SAT'. They wore thick black jackets, military-rate vests, and masked headgear. They possessed a variety of weapons, including Type 89 automatic assault rifles, MP5 submachine guns, and Remington shotguns.

A single cop car cruised its way up the street and parked amongst the cluster of cop cars. Out stepped Chief Mori from the driver's side, dressed in a blue collared shirt with a bullet proof vest overtop.

Officer Hayashi, who stood nearby, walked up to Chief Mori as soon as he saw him.

"So," said Chief Mori, "what's the status, Hayashi?"

"Well, we're waiting on the SAT squad right now. Once they're armed and ready, we'll begin the assault. Oh, look. Here comes their commander now."

One of the SAT officers left the squad and came walking up toward the Chief. He was a tall, built man in his forties with short, buzz-cut black hair. He had a firm expression on his structured face, bearing glasses over his nose.

When the commander stopped in front of the Chief, he fixed his glasses and said, "Hello Chief. The name's Katsu Nishimura. I'm the Commanding Officer of the Tokyo Police Department's Special Unit."

The two men shook hands.

"So here's the plan," Nishimura continued. "My team's going to lead the main assault. It'll be carried out on a floor-by-floor basis. Each time we advance, you and the rest of your department will remain one floor behind. Do not proceed until my team gives the okay."

"Hold on," the Chief interrupted. "Why don't we clear each floor together? Do you really think I'm going to sit and wait for you guys to tell me whether my daughter's safe?"

Nishimura scrunched his face, shifting the position of his glasses.

"We're doing you a favor here, Chief. You'd be risking your life being in the front with us."

"That's the whole point!" the Chief exclaimed. "This is my daughter we're talking about! I'm not going to sit back and wait for someone else to save her. As her father, I have every right to go in there after her; with or without your help."

Commander Nishimura fixed his glasses and turned around.

"Sorry Chief," he said. "In order to ensure your daughter's safety as well as your own, I can't agree to that. Besides, the Special Assault Team's more used to these types of situations than the TPD is."

With that, Nishimura stalked away, rejoining his squad.

"Damn special unit," Chief Mori grumbled to Hayashi. "Always thinking they can order the department around. I'm not so sure they'll be able to handle this case."

"What do you mean, Chief?" asked Hayashi.

"Nothing. It's just, after seeing what happened to those buildings on TV, I'm starting to wonder; what're we dealing with here? I mean, we have no idea what we're up against."

Hayashi placed his hand on the Chief's shoulder

and said, "Don't worry, Chief. I think I can speak for the rest of the department when I say we'll do our best, no matter what it takes, to save your daughter. You're not in this alone."

Chief Mori smiled and nodded, a glint in his eyes.

Then suddenly, an SAT officer surveilling the entrance through a pair night vision binoculars shouted, "We have movement in the lobby!"

"Get into positions!" Nishimura shouted.

Moving with haste, the SAT officers gathered behind the police cars and aimed their guns at the entrance while the TPD officers organized themselves further back.

There was a long silence. Then the front doors swung open.

"Hold your fire!" Nishimura shouted.

Slowly, someone approached out of the darkness, stopping before the entrance with his hands in his pockets. He was a stocky young man, dressed like a typical street punk. The rain drenched his messy black hair, dripping from the tips of his white highlights. He stared at the crowd of officers with a smirk on his face, leering like a predator eying its prey.

"Well, well, well," Kazuo said aloud, "looks like we finally have some visitors. Welcome to the Kanemochi no Hotel my good sirs. What brings you here on this fine, rainy day?"

"You know very well what!" shouted a voice from the back.

The officers turned their heads in alarm; Chief Mori was the one who spoke.

He stared at Kazuo with brooding intensity; then he stalked past his officers.

As the Chief neared the front, Nishimura stopped in his path and said, "Chief, I need you to stay back right now."

Chief Mori shoved the Commander aside and pushed past the SAT squad.

"I know she's in there," he said, flaring his nostrils. "So why don't you save us the trouble and release her? You'd be saving your own life as well."

Kazuo narrowed his eyes and eyed the Chief seriously. Then all of a sudden, he burst out laughing. He bent double and cackled obnoxiously, then raised his head and wiped a tear from his eye.

"Phew, I'm sorry. I just couldn't keep a straight face after hearing that. You're so defiant, Chief Mori. Just like your daughter…"

Chief Mori lowered his head and clenched his fist.

"Just who the hell do you think you are?!" he shouted. "What did she ever do to you? What is it you people want? Money?"

"Please," Kazuo scoffed.

"Well, what then? Was this just a way to get to me?"

Kazuo's face lit up and he bounced his eyebrows.

"But… why?"

Kazuo straightened his face and sighed.

"Alright, Chief. Here's the deal; if you want your daughter to live, you'll follow me inside and head up to the penthouse where we're holding her. There, you and my master shall discuss the terms of her release."

Kazuo held out his hand for Chief Mori to shake.

"What do you say?" he asked, raising his eyebrows.

Chief Mori eyed Kazuo's hand suspiciously.

Then Hayashi emerged from the front and shouted, "Don't listen to him, Chief!"

"Yeah!" shouted another officer. "You don't have to do what he says, Chief!"

Several other officers chimed in.

"We can still rescue your daughter, Chief!"

"Yeah, he's got nowhere to run!"

"Don't trust that punk!"

"Come on, Chief. Don't give into this guy!"

Chief Mori whipped around.

"That's enough!" he shouted.

The officers went silent. Then the Chief turned back to Kazuo with a solemn look on his face.

"I've made my decision," he said, extending his hand.

Kazuo smirked and extended his hand in return. Then suddenly, Chief Mori curled his fingers and punched Kazuo in the stomach.

Damn, thought Kazuo as he hunched over, spit flying from his mouth. *I was not expecting that.*

Kazuo immediately recovered from the blow. Moving swiftly, he seized the arm Chief Mori punched with and put it in a locked position behind the Chief's back. Then he pinned the Chief to the ground, keeping his arm secured with both hands.

All the officers gasped and raised their guns.

"Don't move!" shouted an SAT officer.

Kazuo snickered and hoisted the Chief to his feet, then shoved him forward and dashed back through the entrance, disappearing into the darkness.

The officers eyed the entrance with nervous looks. Meanwhile, the Chief stood behind them with his arms crossed, looking angry. Then there was the loud splashing of someone stomping through a puddle and the Chief turned his head.

Nishimura was standing there, grimacing at the Chief.

"What the hell was that?" he snapped.

The Chief didn't respond. Nishimura shook his head.

"What were you thinking? Are you here to save your daughter or are you here to get yourself killed?"

The Chief narrowed his eyes and advanced toward Nishimura, looking hostile, until Officer Hayashi stepped between them.

"Cool it you two," he mediated. "Have you forgotten why we're here?"

Nishimura snorted at the Chief and stalked back toward the front.

Hayashi looked at the Chief and sighed.

"I will admit, though. That was pretty gutsy what you did back there."

Chief Mori tilted his head back and stared into the sky.

"Sorry," he said. "It's just... this is the most personal case I've ever dealt with. I feel like it's my sole responsibility to solve it. But you're right, Hayashi;

that was foolish of me. I got carried away with my emotions."

Hayashi smiled and placed his hand on the Chief's shoulder.

"I never said you were foolish. What you did made sense. You did what a father should do. I don't think many others would have the courage to do that."

Chief Mori looked at Hayashi with tired eyes and smiled.

"Thanks kid," he said.

"Someone's approaching!" shouted the SAT soldier with the binoculars.

"Ready your weapons!" Nishimura shouted.

The officers regrouped themselves and aimed at the doorway. Then out from the darkness stepped a man in a black kimono with a sheathed katana equipped to his hip.

"What the?" the Chief muttered. "A samurai?"

Ryusuke stopped before the entrance and stared into the crowd with a solemn expression, sweeping the officers with his gaze.

"Disarm your sword and get down on the ground," ordered Nishimura, raising his pistol.

Ryusuke closed his eyes and reached for his katana.

"GET DOWN ON THE GROUND, NOW!" Nishimura shouted, aiming for Ryusuke's head.

But Ryusuke didn't listen; he wrapped his fingers around the hilt and opened his eyes.

Nishimura pulled the trigger and fired, causing the other officers to fire in response.

A storm of bullets shattered the glass doors, creating numerous holes in the wall of the building. However, to the confusion and surprise of the officers, Ryusuke remained still as the bullets rained down on him. His body rippled like the surface of a lake, the bullets whizzing right through him.

The officers gasped in horror. He suffered no wounds, not even a scratch. Not knowing what else to do, they continued to fire.

Then suddenly, Ryusuke vanished.

The officers ceased firing and stared in bewilderment at the spot where Ryusuke had stood.

Then Officer Hayashi felt a sudden searing in his chest. When he looked down, his heart dropped. A long blade jutted from the center of his chest, staining his uniform in blood.

The blade of the katana was transparent with a blue tint. The hilt was metal, but the blade was made of water, compressed together through means of Ryusuke's water manipulation powers.

"Die with honor," Ryusuke whispered into Hayashi's ear. "You shall be the first of many to set forth on the path to the Heavens. Do not fear. You'll be reunited with your comrades soon."

Ryusuke yanked his sword out of Hayashi and a gush of blood burst from the young officer's back. Hayashi stumbled forward and coughed up blood, making a choking sound, and fell onto the asphalt. His limbs convulsed and his fingers twitched as he drew his final breaths.

Every officer, including Chief Mori and Nishimura, gaped in horror at the slaughtering they just witnessed.

"HAYASHI!" Chief Mori bellowed in despair.

Ryusuke flicked the blood off his katana and spoke to the officers.

"The rest of you shall follow your comrade on his journey. I'll extract every one of your souls quickly and painlessly. Be grateful for that. My master's not as gracious as I am."

Nishimura made way past the crowd of officers and confronted Ryusuke. Scowling furiously, he pointed at Hayashi's body and shouted, "You call that gracious, huh? To positions, men!"

Following his order, the SAT squad abandoned their spots at the front and surrounded Ryusuke in a circle, equipping themselves with thicker body armor, headgear, and truncheons.

Ryusuke made a stance with his legs and raised his katana, ready to fight.

Then Nishimura raised his fist in the air, giving the order to advance, and the SAT squad charged at Ryusuke.

As the chaos ensued, Chief Mori backed away toward the entrance. From where he stood, he could see officers pulling out their truncheons and clustering toward the middle, trying to have at Ryusuke, who was being overwhelmed by the SAT squad. However, Ryusuke seemed to have no difficulty holding off on his own. One by one, SAT and TPD officers dropped to the ground, Ryusuke swishing his blade in multiple directions.

Suddenly, the Chief heard a voice from behind.

"Not bad. I didn't expect the Chief of Police to fight dirty."

Chief Mori whipped around to find Kazuo standing there with his hands in his pockets and a smirk on his face.

"You surprised me, I'll give you that much," he continued. "But I can't let that go unnoticed, so what do you say we have some fun?"

Kazuo spread his feet until they were shoulder width apart; then he placed his left foot forward and pulled his right hand back, forming a stance.

"Back when I was just another punk in the streets, I trained hard in the art of Jujitsu until I could hold off on my own. Allow me to give you a demonstration of what I learned."

Kazuo bent the ends of his fingers and delivered a rapid series of palm strikes to Chief Mori's torso. Caught by surprise, Chief Mori painfully received each one of his blows.

Then, in a moment of desperation, he retracted his fist and swung at Kazuo.

Kazuo dodged the punch and grabbed Chief Mori's arm as it was out. Then he turned around and flipped the Chief over his shoulder, sending him crashing down onto the asphalt.

Chief Mori rose to his feet and unstrapped his bullet proof vest, tossing it aside. Then he spread his feet until they were shoulder width apart, turning his right foot sideways while keeping his left foot forward; then he opened his hands and spread his fingers, forming a stance of his own.

Kazuo raised an eyebrow in suspicion.

Hold on, he thought. *I've seen that stance before.*

Paying no mind to it, Kazuo dashed forward and delivered another palm strike.

However, moving with unexpected gracefulness, Chief Mori stepped to the side and avoided the strike. He gripped Kazuo's wrist and rotated it in a circular motion, putting him in a wrist lock; then he yanked Kazuo's hand downward, causing his whole body to lean forward.

With Kazuo's backside exposed, Chief Mori raised his hand and chopped the back of Kazuo's neck, sending him splashing into a puddle.

"Never underestimate your opponent," said Chief Mori. "I've been a master in Aikido for years now."

"Well then," said Kazuo, pushing himself up. "I guess you're not as weak as I thought. In that case..."

Kazuo opened the palm of his right hand and made a clutching motion with his fingers, igniting his blue aura. Chief Mori gasped at the sight of the strange light in Kazuo's hand and stiffened his stance.

Kazuo smirked and continued, "Let's see how you handle my attacks with my evaporation powers thrown into the mix."

16 — THE LILY DESCENDS

Tension filled the air as the three Deaths stood inside the penthouse, glaring at each other silently. Daichi looked down at the floor, watching Mori's unconscious body; then he lifted his head and turned to Maddox.

"Maddox," he said. "My body can't keep this power activated for much longer. Now listen, I need enough energy to get Mori out of here. However, I have enough energy not only to revive you, but to make you three times stronger than Mirko could ever be."

Mirko widened his eyes upon hearing this.

Daichi opened his hands and summoned a white orb in each. They began to spin rapidly, whirring louder and louder.

"And Maddox," said Daichi, "make sure to land a nice one in the jaw for me, alright?"

Maddox smiled and nodded, bracing himself.

With that, Daichi thrust his hands forward and shot two streams of bright energy into Maddox, knocking him off his feet and into the wall.

The blasting lasted a few seconds, the energy building intensely against Maddox; then Daichi closed his hands and the orbs disappeared.

The energy simmered down, becoming less bright, and once it completely diffused, it revealed a sight that made Mirko's heart drop.

Maddox stood there smiling with his arms extended. His face was healed, devoid of any fractures or wounds, and the tatters in his clothes were gone. He walked forward until he faced Mirko; then he took up his fighting stance.

Meanwhile, Daichi walked over to an opening on the floor and jumped in, falling through the water to the floor of the aquarium.

In an attempt to regain control of the situation, Mirko pointed at Maddox and shouted, "What, you think this means you're going to win now?! Just because you got blasted with some power that healed you?! Even if it did give you extra power, that doesn't mean you're stronger! Besides, I still have plenty left in me to defeat you!"

"Mirko," Maddox cut him off, "shut up."

He ignited his flaming fists, and this time, the flames were dark blue in color.

Beneath the floor, Daichi stood at the bottom of the aquarium, staring at Mori's body floating inside the bubble; then he raised his hand and a tender smile formed across his face.

"Let's get out," he said. "You've been trapped here long enough."

The black orb formed in his hand and began to spin, consuming the water in the aquarium.

Meanwhile up above, Mirko raised his hands and resumed his stance, awaiting Maddox's attack. However, Maddox did not move. He just stood there, his fists blazing blue flames.

Hmm, thought Mirko. *This isn't good. With his power increased, and my power decreasing, I'm at a disadvantage. I hate to do this, but if I want to conserve what I have left, I'll have to use something that uses little of my power, but still maintains versatility. It's risky, no doubt, and it'll be tricky, but I have no choice.*

"Well?" said Mirko impatiently, "what are you waiting for? I thought you'd be eager to test your fancy new flames."

Maddox smirked.

"Turn around."

Surprised by his response, Mirko turned around and gasped.

Behind him, a mass of blue fire had taken shape in the form of an animal.

It was fairly large with four legs and hooves, bearing a long face with a snout and two curved horns above its pointed ears. Its thick body was surrounded in bouncing blue flames that resembled fur, and it had two red flames for eyes, giving it an evil, angry look.

Once it finished forming, Mirko raised his eyebrows and laughed.

"Wow," he said sarcastically. "I get it. So this is your 'mad ox', Maddox?"

"Sure is," he said with utter seriousness.

"Wait," Mirko snickered, trying to suppress his laughter, "you're not serious about that thing, are you?"

Maddox glanced at the animal. The Mad Ox huffed, emitting a cloud of smoke through its nose, and charged at Mirko with its head down and horns aimed forward.

It moved with great speed, and just before Mirko could dodge it, the Mad Ox rammed its head into his chest, sending him flying backward.

As Mirko twirled through the air toward Maddox, Maddox retracted his fist, causing the flame to burn brighter, and punched Mirko in the cheek, sending him flying back in the direction of the flaming creature.

The Mad Ox charged again and rammed its head into Mirko's back, shooting him up toward the ceiling. Then the flames of the ox dispersed and the creature disappeared.

Just as Mirko was about to hit the ceiling, he

straightened his legs and kicked off, flying back down toward Maddox.

Maddox scowled and retracted his fist. The flame surrounding his hand formed into a fire ball.

As soon as Mirko was in range, Maddox swung his fist and hit Mirko in the face.

Mirko stumbled back and grabbed his nose, but before he could recover, Maddox dashed forward and unleashed his rage upon Mirko by pummeling him with an endless series of punches.

"This one's for Edmund!" he shouted, hurling his fist into Mirko's stomach.

"This one's for kidnapping Mori!"

He drove his knee into Mirko's crotch.

"And this one's for Daichi!"

He delivered an uppercut to Mirko's chin.

Mirko's head was knocked back from the blow, and he landed on the floor with his limbs sprawled.

Maddox grabbed Mirko by his shirt and hoisted him up, looking him dead in the eye.

"And this," he said, retracting his fist, "is for the Holocaust!"

Maddox released him from his grasp and ambushed him with a series of punches so fast that Mirko had no opportunity to block. Then Maddox ended his attack by delivering one final kick in the stomach which sent Mirko flying back and onto the floor.

For a few moments, Mirko just lay there. However, with difficulty, he managed to stand up, his body heavily bruised and his face bloody.

"Are you finished?" Mirko asked coldly, wiping the blood from his mouth. "Good. Because now I'm going to kill you."

"You sure about that?" asked Maddox, snorting at his words. "You seriously think you can beat me with your powers depleting?"

"You don't *always* need an immense amount of power to kill someone, you know. Sometimes it's the little things that are the most deadly."

Maddox raised an eyebrow.

"Hehe," Mirko chuckled. "I guess there's no point in hiding it. You see, there's a tiny water needle I've placed in your lungs. It's floating inside, waiting to stab upon my command."

Maddox's eyes widened; then his face turned serious and he said, "Bullshit. You think I'm going to buy that?"

"Oh, I wouldn't be so hasty to decide that, Maddox. I may be ruthless, but I'm no liar."

Looking serious, although unsure, Maddox contemplated his options.

No, there's no way that's true. He's trying to toy with me. He has no other options left. Although, he is right; he's no liar. Anytime I doubted him in the past, I always ended up regretting it in the end. Dammit… what should I do?

After a long silence, Maddox finally made his decision. He raised his hands, summoning four flame streams, and shot them at Mirko.

But Mirko didn't move. He just stood there with a smirk.

Suddenly, Maddox felt a sharp pain in his chest and the flames stopped in midair, diffusing away. He hunched over and started hacking into his arm. When he stopped coughing, Maddox looked at his sleeve and gasped; it was stained with blood.

"I told you I wasn't lying," said Mirko. "When I kicked off from the ceiling after your Mad Ox rammed me, I formed a single drop of water in my hand. And then, with an immense amount of precision, I flicked the drop into your mouth and down your windpipe, programming it to form a thin, but deadly needle. It's floating inside your lung as we speak, poised and ready to puncture. I only cut you slightly, but now since you know it's there, next time I won't be so gentle. So what's it going to be, Maddox? You can renounce your powers and leave peacefully, or you can attack again. However if you choose the latter, I won't hesitate to tear you up from the inside."

Maddox stood there in silence, disconcerted by the situation.

A moment later, his mood seemed to ease. He closed his eyes and exhaled. Then he took a deep breath and closed his lips, remaining still.

What's he playing at? Mirko wondered. *Is he devising a method of attack? Or maybe he's come to the conclusion that there's no way out of this. Maybe he's contemplating surrender. Or maybe it's none of those, and he's trying to toy with me, in an attempt to throw off my concentration so as to find an opening.*

Finally, Maddox opened his eyes. Then, without

uttering a word, he turned around and started for the door.

What? He actually decided to surrender? That's not like him at all. Such a shame; I was almost hoping he'd fight ba-

Mirko's thoughts were interrupted when Maddox turned around.

In his mind, Mirko gave the order for the needle to strike. However, when he did so, there was no result; Maddox just stood there, appearing unaffected.

Then Maddox opened his lips and exhaled, releasing a mass of smoke that concealed his presence.

"Why?!" shouted Mirko, his eyes wide with frustration. "Why aren't you dead?!"

The smoke cleared away, gradually revealing an outstretched hand; then Maddox snapped his fingers.

A ball of compressed flames shot from Maddox's finger and raced toward Mirko. Then, upon hitting his chest, it exploded in flames.

In a moment of instinct, Mirko raised his hand and summoned a water shield. However, the explosive force from Maddox's incendiary snap sent Mirko flying back and onto the floor, the shield saving from incineration.

Maddox stepped through the remaining wisps of smoke and stopped before Mirko, who lay on the floor staring in disbelief.

"Impossible!" shouted Mirko. "You should be bleeding your guts out!"

"It wasn't easy, but I was able to evaporate your

little needle. You see, when I closed my eyes and held my breath, I placed all my focus on one part of my body; my lungs. Then I lit a small fire which increased the heat inside. I kept it burning as long as I could, until my lungs could no longer contain the smoke. Luckily, I'm able to keep smoke inhaled longer than most people, since my lungs have basically become accustomed to all the cigarettes I smoke. And thanks to the significant buildup of tar in my lungs, I felt no pain from the flames."

Mirko gritted his teeth in frustration and rose to his feet.

"And so, Mirko," Maddox continued, "once again, your perfect plan has failed."

Maddox extended his arms and snapped his fingers repeatedly, shooting several incendiary flames at Mirko in rapid succession. Mirko summoned a water shield in each hand. Upon impact, the explosions vaporized the water into steam, forcing Mirko to summon a new shield each time.

Maddox advanced forward, snapping faster as he closed in, until he was right on top of Mirko. He moved to snap another incendiary flame, but then Mirko motioned with his hand and summoned a cloud of steam which concealed him.

Maddox stopped in his tracks and gasped. Then suddenly, Mirko darted out of the steam with a long water needle protruding from the tip of his pointer finger, and Maddox felt a sudden piercing in his chest.

He looked down and grunted in pain. The needle

had impaled him through the left side of his chest; straight through his heart. Blood streaked down his clothes from the fresh wound.

Mirko leaned in toward Maddox and spoke into his ear.

"I was ready to take the world by storm, but thanks to you, I doubt that'll happen; all because *you* brought that damn kid along. If it weren't for him, you'd be dead by now. I hope you know that."

Mirko pulled his hand away, extracting the needle, and Maddox dropped to his knees, clutching the wound. Mirko evaporated the needle and lowered his hand.

"Even if I'm not able to stop that kid in my current state, at least I'll have the satisfaction of watching you die. You'll be one less road block on my path to supremacy."

Suddenly, Maddox ignited his aura and a faint red light appeared beneath his hand, followed by wisps of smoke ridden with the stench of burning flesh.

"What the hell are you doing?" asked Mirko.

Then Mirko gasped and his eyes widened.

"Wait a minute," he sputtered. "Don't tell me you're actually trying to cauterize it!"

Maddox lifted his head and glared at Mirko, confirming that he was indeed attempting to seal the wound.

"I can tell it stings," said Mirko. "Wouldn't you rather die than endure that kind of pain?"

"No," Maddox replied, grunting through short breaths. "I'd rather have it sting like a bitch and live than feel nothing and die. I can take it. The pain I feel now doesn't nearly compare to the pain you've caused others."

Amidst his pain and fury, Maddox retracted his hand and ignited his flaming fist; then he slugged Mirko in the gut from where he knelt.

Mirko stumbled back and clutched his stomach.

Then Maddox rose to his feet, his wound fully healed, and said, "Besides, I can't die just yet. I still have an addition to make to my kill count."

He eyed Mirko intensely; then he clenched his fist and summoned a mass of flames that surrounded his entire body.

The flames he summoned were dark blue in color; however, as they burned on, the flames turned to a lighter shade. The flames grew in intensity as the color lightened, becoming brighter, and soon enough, Maddox was engulfed by a massive ball of white flames.

Mirko backed away and shielded his hand over his eyes. The flames burned so bright, it was as if the sun had appeared in the room.

Impossible! thought Mirko. *He managed to summon the white flame?! But something like that should take a lifetime's worth of energy just to summon!*

The spherical mass of white flames began to spin, increasing in speed with each passing second.

Beneath the floor, at the bottom of the aquarium, Daichi's black orb had consumed all the water in the aquarium. However, Mori continued to float midair inside the bubble.

Daichi walked forward until he was standing beneath the bubble; then he raised the orb and touched it against the surface, causing it to pop.

As soon as the bubble burst, Mori dropped through the air. At the same time, Daichi kicked off the ground and shot into the air, catching Mori midflight. As he flew up toward the open tile in the floor above him, he looked down at Mori, who lay asleep in his arms, and gazed admiringly at her face.

Her skin shone brightly from the light, resembling a neatly crafted porcelain doll.

Daichi looked up and kicked through the air, propelling him faster toward the opening.

In the street outside the hotel, the SAT squad and the police pushed on in their battle against Ryusuke.

Ryusuke stood in the center of the street, ten SAT officers surrounding him. One in front charged Ryusuke with a truncheon raised, while two others rushed up from behind, attempting a sneak attack.

However, Ryusuke was well aware of any movement around him. Making use of a police car next to him, he kicked off the hood and leapt into the air.

The three SAT officers stopped in their tracks and looked up. As Ryusuke fell, he made a swift motion with his katana too fast to even see, and when he landed on the ground, the helmeted heads of the officers shot into the air and their decapitated bodies fell to the ground, geysers of blood spurting from their severed necks.

Ryusuke sensed another movement, quite unlike

the motion of a human. It was something small, yet fast and deadly.

He slashed his katana and felt a strong vibration in the hilt, as if something struck the blade. He looked down and saw a dented piece of metal on the ground. Then he looked up. Commander Nishimura was standing there holding a smoking pistol in his hands.

Frightened by the samurai's agility, Nishimura pulled the trigger again.

But Ryusuke was well aware of what he was dealing with. He swished his katana again and deflected the bullet. However, this time he waved his katana in such a motion, the bullet ricocheted back in the direction it was fired from, landing in the left shoulder of the Commander.

Nishimura grunted in pain and dropped the gun, clutching his injured shoulder.

Ryusuke walked over to him; however, he was interrupted when the other seven officers came rushing up from behind, ready to defend their commander.

Ryusuke slid his katana back in his sheathe, then, moving with composed gracefulness, whipped around and darted forward. Rushing for the two officers in the middle, Ryusuke extended his arms and gripped them by their necks; then he dropped to his knees and plunged their heads to the ground. A loud crack like the sound of branches snapping was heard upon impact, and the puddles in the street turned red.

Another officer approached from the left and Ryusuke rose to his feet. He thrust his hand into the officer's stomach. Upon impact, he used his water manipulation powers to liquefy the tissue of the officer's skin, softening it so it could be easily torn or pierced. Paired with great strength, Ryusuke shoved his hand through the officer's gut, shifted around inside; then he yanked it out, holding the officer's stomach.

A waterfall of blood cascaded from the hole in the officer's gut and he collapsed. Meanwhile, another officer approached from the right.

Ryusuke unsheathed his katana and threw the stomach at the helmet of the incoming officer.

Unable to see through the stomach acid staining his visor, the officer was left defenseless as Ryusuke thrust the blade through his neck. At the same time, the three remaining SAT officers darted toward Ryusuke from behind.

Immediately noticing their presence, Ryusuke whipped around and dropped to his knees, arching the blade in a downward motion.

The shifting of the blade's position caused the jugular vein inside the dead officer's neck to rupture and spray blood into the air.

From where he knelt, Ryusuke looked up at the numerous drops of blood raining down on him and muttered, "The rain cleanses, and those who wield it the name of God shall wash away the vermin deemed unworthy by them."

With those words, the drops of blood spraying

from the dead officer's neck directed at the three officers and shot through the air at an incredible speed, piercing through the tops of their helmets as if being peppered by gunfire.

Their bodies dropped to the ground and their limbs convulsed. Then they went still.

Ryusuke removed his katana from the dead officer's neck and gazed at the bodies of his dead enemies. Then his eyes darted to Commander Nishimura, who was stooped over, trying to retrieve his pistol. Unfortunately, his injured shoulder made him unable to do so.

Nishimura could see the samurai approaching through the raindrops staining his glasses. Then his eyes darted to the numerous dead bodies littering the area. It took him a moment; then he came to the horrible realization; Ryusuke had wiped out the entire SAT squad. Any TPD officers who remained kept their distance from the samurai, knowing full well what would happen if they prevented the beast from reaching its prey.

Despite the searing pain from his wound, Nishimura straightened his shoulders in a professional manner and lifted his head, glaring at Ryusuke.

"If you want to live," said Nishimura in a serious tone, "I suggest you back up."

But Ryusuke kept on walking. He raised the blade of his katana.

"You've had your fun," Nishimura pressed on. "This is your last chance, samurai. Back up."

Ryusuke made no form of acknowledgement and continued his strafe.

However, as soon as Ryusuke was within range, Nishimura made a swift, flicking motion with his arm and a small object slid from his sleeve and into his hand.

It was a switchblade, and he held it just inches away from Ryusuke's neck.

"I said back up."

Ryusuke stared blankly at the small blade. There was a long silence; then Ryusuke's eyes met Nishimura's and he spoke.

"Strange... I sense no fear in you. Even as your friends lay dead before you, even as you stare in the face of death, fully aware you have no chance of survival, you do not tremble. I must say, I'm impressed. Even the most valiant warriors' hearts skip a beat before they die."

Ryusuke lifted his hand and a single drop of blood from one of the dead officers rose into the air behind Nishimura.

"Hey," barked Nishimura, raising the blade slightly. "Just what the hell-"

But Nishimura was cut off. With the flicking motion of Ryusuke's hand, the drop of blood shot through the air and struck Nishimura in the back, against his spinal cord.

Nishimura's eyes widened. He stumbled in place, his eyes fluttering, and collapsed.

"You've earned my respect," said Ryusuke to Nishimura's incapacitated body. "For that, I shall allow you to live."

Suddenly, one of the TPD officers raised his gun and fired at Ryusuke, who deflected the bullet with the swish of his blade.

"Everyone!" shouted the officer who fired. "As long as we don't charge him directly, we're safe. Now all of you pull out your guns and fire!"

Amidst their fear and desperation, the remaining TPD officers pulled out their pistols and open fired on Ryusuke.

With reflexes faster than a cat, Ryusuke slashed his blade and deflected the incoming shower of bullets.

As he fended their hail of gunfire, over by the entrance, the battle between Chief Mori and Kazuo ensued.

With his evaporation powers now unleashed, Kazuo darted at Chief Mori and pummeled him with a rapid series of palm strikes. Chief Mori dodged the first few blows; however, on the last attack, he attempted a wrist lock, which ultimately failed when Kazuo moved in and struck Chief Mori in the temple.

Chief Mori stumbled back, feeling lightheaded; then he pulled himself together and resumed his stance.

Kazuo was using a technique of his own design which combined his evaporation powers and the style of Atemi, a technique involving designated strikes to nervous and pressure points, so his attacks would disrupt his enemies' movements while also causing a severe amount of blood loss.

Kazuo returned from his stance and relaxed, sliding his hands into his pockets.

"Hey Chief," he said with a smirk. "Remember that deal I talked to you about earlier? About meeting my superior? Well, guess what? My superior was the one who kidnapped your daughter!"

"Okay," said Chief Mori, sounding uninterested. "I'm still going to fight you, regardless of who kidnapped her."

"That's not what I meant. I'm saying it was never my master's intention to harm your daughter. He took good care of her up in that exquisite penthouse, with the king size bed and flat screen TV. If anything, he treated her like a guest."

"That does not excuse the fact that she was kidnapped. Though, I'm glad to hear she wasn't harmed."

"Oh, I never said she wasn't harmed. I just said she wasn't harmed by my master…"

Chief Mori's eyes narrowed upon hearing this.

Kazuo snickered and darted forward, attempting a strike, but Chief Mori grabbed Kazuo's arm with both hands and redirected the blow downward, causing Kazuo to fall forward and onto the ground.

"Damn, Chief Mori!" said Kazuo, his face against the pavement. "You do it rougher than your daughter!"

He jumped to his feet and resumed his stance, looking like he was about to strike. However, as he made the motion to do so, he retracted his hand abruptly and performed a leg reap instead, making a sideways motion with his leg that caused Chief Mori to trip and fall forward.

As the Chief fell, Kazuo caught him by the collar and pulled him back; then he thrust his hand into the Chief's solar plexus.

Chief Mori grunted in pain, spit flying from his mouth, and stumbled back.

The pain he sustained was more agonizing than any of Kazuo's previous attacks, taking significantly longer for him to recover.

"Just what the hell did you do to her?" he asked through gritted teeth.

"Hehe... she lay there so peacefully. She looked so cute; waking up and looking out the window, wondering where she was and why she was dressed in a nice... spanking... sexy... SLUTTY ASS white bathrobe! I got to say, man, your girl was lookin' DE-LISH!"

Fire in his eyes, Chief Mori let out a raging battle cry and dashed forward, punching at Kazuo's face. However, Kazuo blocked the punch; then he gripped Chief Mori's arm and overturned it, forcing him into an arm lock.

"Come on now," said Kazuo. "I thought Aikido was supposed to be a defensive style of fighting. If you keep letting your anger get the best of you, this will be over very soon."

Kazuo released him and attempted another strike to the solar plexus, but Chief Mori was prepared this time. He gripped Kazuo by the wrist and drove his

216

elbow downward to crush his arm. However, Kazuo anticipated this and gripped Chief Mori's wrist with his free arm, stopping his elbow strike; then he swung Chief Mori's arm over and around his head, throwing him down.

Kazuo stifled a laugh as he watched Chief Mori push himself up.

"I'll admit she did have a nice ass," Kazuo continued. "Although I must say she could use a little more work in the tits."

Once again, Chief Mori rushed to attack Kazuo, but his attempts were futile; Kazuo dropped to one knee and used his hands to send the incoming Chief flying over his head.

"After your daughter woke up, I told her she didn't have much to look at. Of course, she responded by throwing a shoe in my face."

Chief Mori let out a small chuckle.

"Sounds like my daughter, all right," he said.

"Hehe… well, I didn't respond too well after that. Actually, I'd say I reacted rather violently… wasn't a pretty sight."

Chief Mori's face turned serious.

"Listen up you little prick," he said darkly "What ever the hell you did to my daughter, I swear I'm going to-"

"What? Make me pay? Kill me? Go on then. I'd like to see you try."

Kazuo rushed forward, ignited the blue aura in his hands, and battered every part of Chief Mori's body with a multitude of strikes, packing a tremendous amount of force into each.

Having become severely dehydrated from the evaporation powers implemented into Kazuo's attacks, Chief Mori became lightheaded and his movements slowed. In a desperate attempt to regain control of the fight, Chief Mori threw a punch to Kazuo's face. But it was a sluggish punch, and Kazuo took advantage of it.

With one hand, he gripped Chief Mori by the wrist and spun in place, lifting him off his feet and into the air, swinging his body in a circle. Then finally, Kazuo let go, sending Chief Mori smashing into the side of the hotel.

Kazuo stalked over to where Chief Mori lay and hoisted him by the collar of his shirt.

Chief Mori looked beaten and disheveled; his were clothes soaked, and he had bruises all over his face.

"You know what I did to her after she threw the shoe at me?" Kazuo continued. "I grabbed her by the neck and unleashed my powers on her. Ah, if only you had seen the look in her eyes; so full of fear. She was like a scared little animal trembling in the clutches of its predator. I doubt she knew what was happening at first, but once she became lightheaded from the blood loss, it didn't take long for her to figure out. I must say, out of all the people who I've dehydrated to death, she succumbed the quickest. Unlike you, she didn't even put up a fight. All she did was stare at me, quivering with wide eyes as I brought her closer to death."

Kazuo released Chief Mori and delivered several strikes to his chest and face, finishing with a strike to the shoulder which sent Chief Mori stumbling backwards in a circle. But Kazuo didn't let Chief Mori go far. He grabbed him by the arm and pulled him back. Then he extended his arm out to the side.

Chief Mori's face made contact with Kazuo's arm and he was knocked to the ground.

Kazuo looked down at him and spoke with a big grin, "I was so close to killing her. Then my master entered the room just as she was about to lose feeling in her neck. Of course, he told me to stop because he needed her alive. It's hilarious, isn't it?! My master, the one who kidnapped your daughter, ended up being the one who saved her! Had he not interfered when he did, your daughter would have died right then and there! If you think about it, Chief, I'm the only one who's actually tried to kill her!"

Chief Mori pushed himself up; however, there was no expression on his face. Any irritation or hostility from before was absent. He appeared calm and composed, quite unlike the tempered, headstrong person he was a minute ago.

The two spaced themselves from each other and Kazuo took up his stance again.

Chief Mori closed his eyes and took a deep breath, putting his hands together as if he were praying. Then he opened his eyes, taking up his Aikido stance, and said, "Now I'm ready to give it my all."

Kazuo and Chief Mori stared each other down for what seemed like an eternity. Then Kazuo made the first move. He charged forward and attempted a palm strike to Chief Mori's chest, but the Chief didn't move a muscle; not until Kazuo's hand was just inches away.

He turned to his side, gripping Kazuo's wrist, and pulled downward. Taking advantage of Kazuo's momentum, Chief Mori used his other hand to flip Kazuo by pressing against his stomach.

Kazuo landed on his backside then immediately jumped up, resuming his stance.

He darted forward again and attempted a round-house kick. Chief Mori moved to the side, grabbed Kazuo by his ankle, and yanked upwards, throwing him off balance. Then he slammed his elbow against Kazuo's leg and knocked him to the ground.

Kazuo bolted back up and grabbed Chief Mori's arm. However, when he tried attempting a lock, he was unable to move Chief Mori's arm from its position.

Then Chief Mori made a wide circular motion with his arm, lifting Kazuo off his feet, and thrashed him against the ground.

Kazuo rose to his feet, his face full of frustration, and darted for the Chief again.

Chief Mori intercepted Kazuo's incoming strike by grabbing his wrist and flipping him over.

Kazuo attempted to attack repeatedly, but every time, Chief Mori would just redirect the blow and flip him.

Kazuo pushed himself up, his face bruised from the many times he made contact with the pavement, and scowled at Chief Mori, who had not moved an inch from where he stood since he came to.

Kazuo cracked his knuckles and dashed forward. But this time, he wrapped his arm around Chief Mori's arm and pulled down, attempting a joint lock. However, once again, Kazuo was unable to move the Chief's arm from place.

Chief Mori swung his arm through the air, hurtling Kazuo along with him, and smashed him face-down to the ground. Kazuo tried breaking away, but just in time, Chief Mori grabbed Kazuo by the wrist and overturned his body.

"The more you struggle," said Chief Mori, thrashing Kazuo again. "The more momentum you're providing me to flip you."

Every time Kazuo tried squirming away, Chief Mori would just toss him again. Then finally, after being manhandled into the pavement numerous times, Kazuo stopped struggling.

"Alright, alright!" he shouted, smacking his hand against the ground. "You win!"

Chief Mori released Kazuo and stepped back, allowing him to stand up.

Kazuo glared at the Chief, looking beaten and defeated, and wiped the blood from his nose.

"The cuffs, Chief," he said sourly, holding out his hands. "Take me in."

As the Chief reached for his pants, a devious smile formed on Kazuo's face and he dashed forward.

"PSYCH!" he shouted, attempting a strike.

The Chief reacted instantly. With his left hand, he

redirected the strike downward, and with his right hand, landed a punch on the side of Kazuo's face.

Kazuo flew backwards, twirling through the air, and landed facedown. This time, he didn't get up.

"Damn street punks," grumbled Chief Mori, brushing his shoulders. "Where do they get off fighting dirty like that?"

Chief Mori looked over at the officers in the street and saw they were still firing at Ryusuke.

Slowly, the number of bullets lessened. One by one, the officers stopped firing and craned their heads. Soon enough, everyone in the street, including Ryusuke, was staring at the top of the hotel.

The windows of the penthouse were blazing with light, as if a hundred spotlights were flashing inside. The intensity of the beams increased then decreased like it was pulsing, its rays extending to the far reaches of the horizon.

Chief Mori narrowed his eyes and muttered, "What the hell is going on up there?"

Then the beams stopped pulsing. Instead, they grew bigger and brighter, until they were so bright, the officers had to shield their eyes.

Suddenly, the light retracted back into the penthouse, and then, the top of the hotel exploded, bursting into flames.

The front section creaked and groaned with the scraping sound of metal against metal. Then there was a shower of sparks and the front section at the top gave way, lurching forward. As the mass of debris plummeted from above, Chief Mori noticed a glowing figure falling amidst the rubble, holding someone in its arms.

Daichi held Mori tight with one hand and summoned the black orb in the other, which consumed the surrounding debris, breaking the material down into an ocean of particles which swirled through the air and shimmered, trailing into the orb like a swarm of fireflies.

By the time Daichi landed before the entrance, all the debris was gone.

Chief Mori, the officers, and Ryusuke stared in disbelief as to what they just witnessed.

The Chief was especially shocked to see Daichi with a strange aura surrounding his body, his daughter asleep in his arms. He didn't know whether to be relieved or scared.

Daichi lifted his head and looked Chief Mori in the eye, a serious expression on his face. Then he craned his head, pointed his finger up, and shot a black orb into the sky. At first there was nothing. Then there was a loud whoosh and the rainclouds gathered together, swirling above the hotel and disappearing away.

On the rooftop of the building next to the hotel, Shinji stared into the sky and for once, actually showed emotion when he raised his eyebrows. It was difficult to tell whether he was surprised or impressed.

In less than a minute, the rain had stopped, and the light from sun began to break through.

Down below, Kazuo came to. He sat up, rubbed

his forehead, and opened his eyes.

He awoke to the sight of Daichi surrounded by his unusual aura, holding the Chief's daughter in his arms. Then he looked up and saw the top of the hotel in flames. He gasped and rose to his feet; then he looked over at Ryusuke.

The two nodded firmly to each other and slowly approached the threat before them, until Kazuo was interrupted by the ringing of his cell phone. He snatched it out of his pocket and answered it.

"What is it?" he snapped, sounding agitated.

"Get out of there; both of you."

It was Kasami's voice.

"Hell no!" barked Kazuo. "The little prick has the girl!"

"Listen to me! I've experienced his power for myself. You and Ryusuke don't stand a chance."

"Hold on, are you saying you've fought this punk already?"

"He defeated me, Kazuo."

"What?!"

"You heard me. We need to fall back. Now grab Ryusuke before he goes samurai on his ass and get yourselves out of there. Meet me at the rendezvous point. There's still a possibility that the master survived."

Swallowing his pride, Kazuo looked back at Ryusuke and shook his head.

Ryusuke stopped walking. Then he sheathed his katana and nodded back.

With that, the two Shinigami left the scene. None

of the officers bothered to stop them; their attention was fixed on Daichi.

Finally, Mori awoke. She opened her eyes and gasped at the sight of Daichi, too overwhelmed to speak. She lay there still, staring at him curiously.

Chief Mori, unaware his daughter was awake, took a step forward and reached out his hand.

"D-Daichi?" he stuttered hesitantly.

Daichi smiled.

"Relax, Chief," he said.

Chief Mori stopped in his tracks and stared. Never had he heard Daichi speak like this before.

"She's safe now."

Daichi turned around and headed through the entrance.

No one knew how to react. One of the officers pulled out his gun and raised it timidly. But then, Chief Mori placed his hand over the barrel and lowered it. The officer looked at him quizzically, but the Chief shook his head.

Daichi stepped through the entranceway and entered the lobby, the glow of his aura illuminating the dim room; then he walked up to the fountain and lowered Mori to her feet next to it.

"Um… Daichi?" she began.

But Daichi didn't acknowledge her. He sat himself on the floor, resting his back against the base of the fountain, and closed his eyes.

Mori dropped to her knees, placed her hand on his shoulder, and leaned in toward his face.

"Daichi?" she whispered, shaking his shoulder.

"Are you alright?"

Slowly, his white and black aura began to fade away, the color returning to his skin, clothes, and the rest of his body. Then he opened his eyes and grunted, sitting himself up.

"What the?" he mumbled, glancing around the room. "How'd I end up back in the lobby?"

Noticing Mori's hand on his shoulder, he turned his head and looked up at her.

"Mori!" he exclaimed, sounding relieved. "Oh, thank goodness you're alright! How the heck did you make it out of there?"

Mori raised an eyebrow.

"You don't remember?" she asked.

"Last thing I remember was Kasami-"

He stopped midsentence and gasped.

"That's right!" he said. "Kasami killed me! But then how…?"

He stared at his hands, trying to recall what happened, but he couldn't remember.

He shook his head. Then he looked at Mori and said, "So anyways, Mori, tell me. How'd you escape?"

Mori was silent for a moment. Then she smiled.

"*You* saved me, Daichi."

"I-I did?"

Mori giggled; then she reached forward and threw her arms around him.

"Yes, Daichi," she said softly into his ear. "You did save me, and I don't know what I would have done had you not. He told me some pretty crazy stuff;

Mirko I mean. For a while, I felt like I was really going to die in there. But… you kept me going, Daichi. I had a feeling it'd be you, my father, or Tsubaki who'd save me. But I could tell it was going to be you, because… well… I wanted it to be you, Daichi."

Daichi was at a loss for words. He blushed, gazing at her smiling face, and listened silently as she continued.

"Remember when we were younger you told me about how much you wanted to have Middlemist Red Camellias in your garden? Well, yesterday after school, I stopped by the flower shop I usually pass on the way home, and they had one Middlemist Red Camellia bush left in stock. Guess what I did when I saw it."

"You didn't buy them, did you?"

"I did. I brought it home with me and I was going to give it to you today when I came over. But then all this happened, and they're probably shriveled up by now. It's a shame; I really wanted you to see them."

Then Daichi gasped. He remembered back when he stumbled upon a pot of Middlemist Red Camellias on the seventy-ninth floor, and how he chose to fight Kasami because she killed them with her steam.

As soon as he pieced it together, Daichi wrapped his arms around Mori and held her close.

"Don't worry," he responded into Mori's ear. "I've seen them. And they were beautiful, Mori; more beautiful than I imagined them to be, and more beautiful than any flower I've ever laid eyes on.

I'm sorry I couldn't protect them in time. But don't worry, I've avenged their deaths and their killer got what for."

Mori had no idea what he was talking about, but she didn't care. She just wanted to enjoy the moment and stay embraced in his arms.

"I couldn't live without you," he continued. "You may be one flower in a field of many, but it takes two flowers to create a new one, and there's no other flower I'd rather choose than you. You're colorful, you smell nice, and when you bloom, you outshine all the others. But what makes you most special is that you're always by my side, giving me shade when the heat of the sun is beating down. And if I were ever to fall, you were prepared to fall with me. You kept *me* going, Mori. Without everything you've done, I'd be lost in a world of despair. Without you, I would have shriveled up and died a long time ago."

Outside the building, the storm had cleared and the sun was out, casting rays of sunlight through the crevices in the wall upon the two embraced figures before the fountain.

Mori closed her eyes and clung to Daichi silently. Meanwhile, Daichi's eyes shifted downward and he gasped, his face blushing red.

"Um, Mori," he mumbled. "Not trying to sound weird or anything, but your bathrobe's kind of um… open."

Mori looked down and her cheeks flushed bright red; then she leapt to her feet and covered herself.

"Sorry," she said bashfully, retying her bathrobe.

Suddenly, they were interrupted by the sound of footsteps coming from the doorway. Daichi and Mori whipped around to see who was there and gasped; Chief Mori was approaching them.

Mori's face lit up with a huge smile and she ran into his arms.

"Father, you came!"

"Of course I did, sweetheart," he said, smiling. "Your kidnapper's been taken care of. And don't worry about that guy who threw the shoe at your face. I gave him what for."

"You fought him?!" she exclaimed, looking concerned. "Are you okay? He didn't do anything to you, did he? How does your head feel? You're not lightheaded, are you?"

"Calm down, Mizuki," he reassured, patting her on the shoulder. "I know what he's capable of. But don't worry. It'll take a whole lot more than that to bring me down."

"I know, but you should at least see a doctor, just to make sure you're alright."

Chief Mori chuckled and gave her a hug.

"Always so concerned for me, just like your mother. Alright, since you said so, I'll stop by the hospital as soon as my men are finished up here, just as long as you see a doctor too."

"But father, I'm fine."

"Aha, see?" he chortled.

Chief Mori lifted his head; when his eyes met with Daichi's, his face turned serious. Carefully, he let go of his daughter and walked past her, confronting

Daichi.

They stared at each other for what seemed like an eternity. Then finally, Chief Mori spoke.

"I don't know what the hell you and Maddox are up to, but it's clear you're hiding something. I'm assuming those buildings received damaged from when you fought the kidnappers. And by looks of it, you two were the ones who sent the top of this building crashing down. That evidence alone is enough for me to put you in jail."

Daichi gulped and held his position.

Mori didn't know what to say, but she wasn't prepared to let Daichi take the blame.

"However," Chief Mori continued, his face easing slightly, "you are also the one who rescued my daughter. And even though my officers and I were almost killed by that debris, you protected us by making it disappear. You did as you and Maddox said you would; you saved the life of the person who means the most to me in this world. I thank you for that, and I don't know how I can ever repay you. Although, I think we can agree that putting what you did behind us would be the best choice for now."

Daichi attempted a smile and nodded.

"Very well then," said Chief Mori, walking toward the exit, placing his arm around his daughter. "We'll settle this matter for another day, Daichi Hara. However…"

He stopped before the exit and turned back around.

"Should you ever do something with your powers

that gets my daughter involved, or puts her in danger in any way, next time I won't be so forgiving."

"I understand, sir."

Just as Chief Mori was about to leave, he stopped again.

"Oh shit!" he exclaimed. "Speaking of Maddox, where is he? He didn't get caught in that explosion, did he?"

"Don't worry," Daichi reassured. "I'm sure he's fine."

Chief Mori raised an eyebrow.

"Trust me," Daichi chuckled. "It'll take a lot more than that to kill him."

Unscathed from his own explosion, Maddox descended the emergency stairwell and reached into his pocket, pulling out a pack of cigarettes.

He grabbed a cigarette from the pack and placed it between his lips; then he snapped his fingers and lit a flame to it.

"Hmm," he said, taking a puff. "It's pretty humid out today."

A trail of smoke followed him down the stairwell.

17 — AN ILLEGITIMATE HEIR

A day had passed since the incident at the Kane-mochi no Hotel. It was Monday and the sun hung in the center of the clear blue sky, the cherry blossoms blooming on the trees surrounding the grounds of Kurosaki High School.

Classes had ended over an hour ago. However, most of the students stayed after to watch the bas-ketball game, for today was the finals of the Kanto Region Tournament, and Kurosaki High's Basket-ball Team was to compete against Yagami High in the gym. The team to win would be the one to advance to the Interhigh Championship, where they'd compete against teams in other regions of Japan.

Inside the gym, the bleachers were packed to the brim with students along with family members of the participating players. Most of the girls were amassed at the front so they could get a good view of Kurosaki's star point guard Yunano Tsubaki.

The last quarter had just begun; the score was 63 to 61 with Yagami in the lead, and the shooting guard for Yagami had just stolen a pass made by Kurosaki's power forward.

Drops of sweat flew from the players' faces as they sprinted down the court, struggling to keep their team's lead.

Yagami's shooting guard made it past the three-point arc with the ball, and was well on his way to the basket with no one in the way. He made the motion to pass the ball to his team's center, who was right beneath the basket, until suddenly, Tsubaki dashed out of nowhere and stole the ball.

With Tsubaki in possession of the ball, he knew he had to pass it to one of the players by the net to get the two points to tie it up. But it wouldn't be an easy attempt. His team's shooting guard and center were both being blocked by Yagami players, and the power forward was on the opposite side; too far to make a clean pass.

He made it past the midcourt line. Then suddenly, Yagami's small forward appeared in front of him, blocking his path.

He was a spry-looking kid, athletic and full of energy. Just by looking at him, Tsubaki could tell he wouldn't be easy to fool.

So instead, Tsubaki chose an alternative move. With precise speed and agility, he zigzagged past three of Yagami's players, making it past the three point arc, and performed a layup shot which made it into the basket, tying the game.

The girls in the stands jumped and cheered as Tsubaki returned to the center of the court, brushing the sweat off his forehead.

Meanwhile, Daichi sat alone at the top of the bleachers, looking dreary and exhausted. He sighed and slouched his shoulders, slumping forward.

As he sat there, reflecting on the events that ensued a day ago, his frame of mind was suddenly interrupted by a familiar voice.

"Hey."

He knew that voice anywhere.

He turned his head to see Mori, who had sat herself down next to him.

The two stared ahead in silence, until finally, Mori spoke.

"Daichi," she said, "don't let what my father said get to you. You know how he is. He can be really overprotective sometimes."

"But he's right. If something ever did happen to you, I'd never forgive myself."

"Why would something happen to me?"

"I don't know. It's just, after what happened with Mirko, I'm afraid someone'll try to use you like that again."

"I'm the daughter of the Chief of Police, Daichi. There's always going to be that possibility."

Daichi didn't respond.

"I know what you are," she continued. "Mirko told me everything; what you have to do as a Death, and the powers you're given to do it. But that doesn't make you a monster, and even though I think it's terrible, it's not going to change how I feel about you."

Mori placed her hand over Daichi's hand.

"No matter what happens," she continued, smiling gently, "I'll never let this power bring you down. Ever since we were kids, we've always been there for each other. And that's not about to change, no matter what my dad says."

Lightened by her words, Daichi looked up at her and attempted a smile.

The two gazed at each other; then they stared ahead, watching as Tsubaki zigzagged past two opposing players and made a pass to his team's small forward, who received the ball and made a three-point shot into the basket.

"Looks like Tsubaki's going all out for this game," said Mori.

"Eh," Daichi shrugged. "He's trying to hog all the attention."

"I don't think so. He takes his games pretty seriously. One day, he's going to become pro."

Daichi chuckled obnoxiously.

"Yeah!" he snickered. "And I can't wait to see the look on his father's face when he does!"

Mori gave Daichi a disapproving look.

"You shouldn't joke about that. You know how things are between him and his father."

"Wait, are you telling me he hasn't moved back in with his family yet? Is he *still* living in that apartment complex?"

"Yeah. He told me he won't return until his family accepts him for who he is."

"What'd he mean by that?"

"Well, he has three older brothers, and I hear they don't approve of Tusbaki's choosing to pursue basketball. He's also the bastard child of the family. He was born from a different mother, so they don't really treat him as an equal."

"I knew that, but why are his brothers so against basketball?"

"Well, his oldest brother Keijiro is the vice president of their father's pharmaceutical corporation, and he's only thirty. Tsubaki doesn't say much about his brothers, but I've heard little things about them. His second oldest brother is a lawyer who has his own firm, and he's only twenty-three. And the third oldest is eighteen and in medical school, training to become a neurosurgeon."

"Wow," nodded Daichi. "They've made it far for their age."

"Yeah."

Mori lifted her shoulders and sighed.

"Poor Tsubaki. It takes dedication to do what you love even though your family doesn't appreciate you for it."

Thinking on Mori's words, Daichi stared ahead and watched as Tsubaki dribbled the ball across the court, putting his all into the game. Then he turned to Mori and rose to his feet.

"I'm going down to take a closer look," he said.

He stepped down the bleachers and stood on the floor, next to the stands. From where he stood, he could see Tsubaki's precise footwork as he dodged the opposing players' attempts at stealing the ball.

As Tsubaki neared the basket, the crowd went into an uproar, including Daichi, who cupped his hands around his mouth and bellowed, "Come on, Tsubaki! You got this!"

Tsubaki chuckled to himself when he heard Daichi's cry amongst the others.

However, as he passed the midcourt line, Yagami's point guard approached him from the side and swung at the ball. It looked like he was about to steal it, but then, Tsubaki switched the ball to his other hand and passed the ball to Kurosaki's power forward, who was open on the opposite side.

The power forward received the ball successfully and made a shot from behind the three point arc. The ball bounced off the backboard, spun around the rim twice, then fell into the basket.

Everyone in the bleachers jumped up and cheered. The score was 70 to 68 with Kurosaki in the lead, and there were only five minutes left on the clock.

Suddenly, Daichi heard a loud, bellowing voice in his left ear.

"Eh, that was a cheap shot!"

Daichi turned his head in bewilderment, wondering who in the world dared to speak bad about his team.

Standing next to Daichi was the biggest high school student he had ever seen. He was a strapping boy with meaty hands and muscular arms, with biceps as thick as tree logs. He towered over Daichi with an impressive height of 6'4. He had shoulders broad as clubs, and above his six-pack, it looked like he had two steel plates for a chest. While his upper body was built and bulky, from the waist down he was somewhat slim. He had short, slick black hair above his large forehead, and beneath his slightly hooked nose, he had a long, structured chin, resembling that of a superhero's.

Daichi eyed the emblem on the boy's green and yellow colored sport jacket. It was two red boxing gloves punching together; the logo of the Kurosaki High Boxing Team.

Standing there with his arms crossed, the boy watched the game with a disapproving glare.

"I mean really," he muttered to himself. "He only made the shot cause of that lucky pass the point guard made."

"So what if it was lucky?!" shouted Daichi.

The boy turned his head in alarm.

"That wasn't luck," Daichi pressed on. "That point guard there's a friend of mine. I've seen him outfox players like that millions of times. And buddy, let me tell you, what he did was not an easy thing to do. You call that luck? No, that's skill."

The boy stared at Daichi with wide eyes, unsure what to say. Then his face eased and he grinned.

"Do you know who you're talking to, kid?" he said in a gruff voice.

"Nope," Daichi responded simply. "And I don't care. Especially if you think you can talk smack about my friend. The only person who gets to talk smack about him is me."

"Hehe," the boy chuckled. "You've got balls, I'll give you that. The name's Hiroto Saito. And I'm the best boxer Kurosaki has to offer. So for future reference, don't mess with me, unless of course you're an idiot."

"Wait a minute! You're on the boxing team for Kurosaki High, yet you're rooting *against* its basketball team?"

"I got some buddies over at Yagami, and some of them are out there playing right now. But that's not the only reason I'm rooting for them. I've been to every one of their games this season, and I got to say, they've really been pushing themselves this year. In my opinion, they deserve that spot in the Interhigh more than anyone else in the region."

"How could you say that?" Daichi exclaimed, stepping closer. "Kurosaki's been pushing themselves too, you know. They've got some really good players on their team this year. The coaches say Masaru's one of the fastest small forwards they've ever seen. Same goes for their center Kyoya. He broke the school record last year for most slam dunks in the season. And don't even get me started on the star point guard of Kurosaki High."

"See, that's the problem," continued Hiroto. "Kurosaki's only good because of those 'star' players. If they're so good, how come you didn't mention the other two?"

"Who, you mean Akio and Goro? They're alright, but they're nowhere near as good as Masaru, Kyoya, or Tsubaki. But you can't really blame them since they only joined the team this year."

"See, that's their weakness," Hiroto went on. "Kurosaki's like a scale that has too much weight on one end and not enough weight on the other, whereas Yagami is perfectly balanced. Kurosaki focuses on utilizing their players' individual talents, while Yagami focuses more on working together as a team. Now yes, it is good to strengthen your players' skills, but you need to be able to blend them together, regardless of how good they are. You got to try out different systems until you find one that best suits your team. And that is the most important step which every high school seems to miss."

"Yeah, well systems don't always work now, do they?!" Daichi burst out loudly, clenching his fist. "Sometimes, you'll have a good team, and everyone'll do their job the way they're supposed to. But there will always be that one player who thinks he's better than everyone, who thinks he can manipulate the game, the world, and everyone around him!"

People in the crowd started to stare. There was a dark look in Daichi's eyes. Hiroto stared in shock, not knowing what to say.

"That one bad egg in the bunch," continued Daichi, "who thinks it's okay to take the people you care about and use them for his own selfish benefit! And after it all, once you've beaten him, you begin to wonder what drove him to do all this in the first place. And even more so, you wonder… could that end up being me in the future? If I keep this game going long enough, to the point where I become just as good a player as he was, will that alter my personality as well? Will I change and become the monster that he was?"

For a moment, Daichi stood with his head down, lost in his emotions. Then he snapped out of it and looked around.

Hiroto didn't know what to say or how to react. Normally, he would have slugged him in the gut by now, but deep down, he could tell there was something more to all this; something he couldn't put his finger on.

Daichi, embarrassed by the situation, looked away from Hiroto and walked off.

After he disappeared through the exit door, everyone's attention reverted back to the game, aside from Hiroto, who stood there pondering Daichi's words. Then his mixed thoughts were interrupted by a familiar voice from behind him.

"Holy shit, Hiroto. Was that Daichi Hara?"

Hiroto turned around and his expression eased.

"Oh, 'sup Tetsuo. You know that kid?"

"Know him? Hells yeah, I know him. He's a punk, a pussy, and a stuck up, bratty-mouthed little bitch.

What of it? The little punk givin' you trouble?"

Hiroto thought on it for a moment.

"Not sure," he said.

"Well, I'll make sure he doesn't give you any more, then."

Hiroto raised an eyebrow.

As soon as the basketball game ended, the exit doors swung open and the crowd filed out. Some headed down the hallway and left the building, while some hung out in the corridors, talking amongst themselves.

Daichi stood at the corner of the hallway, leaning against the wall with a tired look on his face, shadows under his eyes. When Mori came out, he straightened himself and eased his expression.

"Hey you!" said Mori teasingly. "Where'd you run off to?"

"Uh… the bathroom."

"Oh. Well, you missed the rest of the game, silly!" She punched Daichi's arm playfully.

"Hey," Daichi chortled. "I had to go. Besides, I'm sure we'll get an earful from Tsubaki-"

"Hey Hara!" boomed a loud voice, echoing across the hallway.

Daichi and Mori turned their heads simultaneously.

Standing down the hallway were three boys dressed in green and yellow sport jackets like Hiroto's. They all looked the same age as Daichi. However, each one of them was built differently.

The one in the center was the tallest of the three; well-built with a muscular upper body. His spiky blond hair stood straight on the top of his head. Upon his sharp chin was a small tuft of blond facial hair, and around his neck he wore a gold chain necklace. The front of his jacket bore a picture of two hockey sticks crossed together; the emblem of the Kurosaki High Hockey team. And next to it was a gold star, signifying that he was the captain. A nasty smirk rid his smooth, handsome face as he glared at Daichi with narrowed eyes.

The one on the left was the second tallest. He was thin and he had wavy brown hair parted down the middle. His jacket bore a picture of a bat with a baseball in front of it; the emblem of the Kurosaki High Baseball Team. His nostrils flared as he glared at Daichi with his arms crossed.

The one on the right was the shortest of the three. He was small and scrawny, with blond hair gelled to the side with black highlights. He wore several bracelets around his wrists, and his jacket bore a picture of two figures grappling each other by the arms; the emblem of the school's wrestling team, with a captain's star by its side. Standing with his thumbs in his pockets, he snorted at Daichi and sniggered.

The one in the middle was the one who had spoken. Students in the hallway moved aside to let the boys through. Everyone stopped their conversations and murmured to each other in hushed voices.

"Heads up, it's them."

"You mean the big three?"

"I hope they're not up to something."

"I don't know, but Tetsuo looks like he means business."

The boy in the middle spoke.

"Well, well, well. It's been a while, Hara."

As Daichi watched him speak, he remembered back to the day in grade school when a group of three boys tried beating him up, and Mori came to save him.

These boys were the Taniguchi Brothers, with Toshio on the right, Tsuneo on the left, and Tetsuo in the middle.

"What do you want?" Daichi asked bitterly.

The three brothers sniggered in unison.

"What do you waaaant?" Toshio repeated in a nasal voice.

"Yup, he's still dumb as ever," Tsuneo remarked.

Daichi crossed his eyebrows and stepped forward.

"HEY!" he shouted.

The Taniguchis, along with everyone else in the hallway, went silent.

"Toshio," Daichi began. "Still as childish as ever, I see. Mimicking people like a first grader does. And Tsuneo, aren't you embarrassed by the fact that both your brothers are captains and you're not? I mean, come on. Your squat little brother Toshio makes captain of the *varsity wrestling team*, while you get stuck playing on the JV baseball team? That's sad."

Inciting "oohs" and gasps were heard from the crowd.

Their tempers flaring, Toshio and Tsuneo advanced toward Daichi, looking hostile.

"Don't," Tetsuo ordered.

Toshio and Tsuneo stopped in their tracks and turned around.

"Aw, come on!" Tsuneo whined.

"Yeah Tets', let us have at him!" urged Toshio.

"Hold on just a minute, boys."

Tetsuo looked up at Daichi and scowled.

"Daichi, Daichi, Daichi," he sighed, shaking his head. "You haven't changed a bit. Ever since we were kids, you always had an act for pissing people off; talking big, acting like you know everything. But we know the truth. We know full well that Mori goes out of her way to help you study!"

Mori scowled and took a step forward with her fists clenched.

"Ah!" exclaimed Tetsuo, his face lighting up. "Speak of the devil, it's the tutor herself!"

Mori glared silently at Tetsuo.

"Why do you hang with this guy, Mori?" Tetsuo continued, raising an eyebrow. "I mean, let's face it. You're hot, and he's not."

He smiled and extended his arms.

"Come on Mori, how 'bout it? Want to date a *real* man?"

"Piss off," she spat.

Tetsuo's smile vanished.

"Shit, she told you, Tets'!" teased Tsuneo.

"Hmm," said Toshio to Mori. "Looks like you've caught Daichi's attitude. I guess that's what you get for hanging around him so much."

Mori was about to deliver a retort, but then, Daichi grabbed her shoulder and pulled her back. When she looked up at him, he had a dark look in his eyes and a grimace on his face.

"Daichi…?"

"Stay back, Mori."

He didn't even look at her when he spoke; he just glared ahead at the sniggering Taniguchis.

"Daichi, you don't have to-"

"No," he said firmly. "Let me handle this."

He walked forward and approached the Taniguchis with hostility in his posture. Then he stopped in front of Tetsuo and looked him in the eye.

"Tetsuo," he began, "I'm betting you're a pretty good hockey player, considering you made team captain. However, even though you're good at hockey, you're also good at being a real douchebag."

More "oohs" and gasps were heard from the crowd.

While this ensued, Haruka Tsukino stood amongst the crowd, watching Daichi in particular.

Jeez, she thought, observing the solemn look on his face. *I've never heard him speak like that before. He sounds so assertive; nothing like how he was the other day. Something about him's changed. I can't describe it, but… it's kind of awesome.*

Once the reactions from the crowd died down, Daichi continued, "I remember hearing about you last year… oh yeah. It was when you broke the school's record for most participated fights in one game. Yeah… you think you're better than everyone, don't you? You think just because you're good, you're allowed to belittle anyone you find inferior. And in your mind, you think that's what makes a good leader. Well Tetsuo, if that's what you think, then you're mistaken. A good leader is not one who takes advantage the weak. A good leader is one who nurtures the weak and makes them stronger."

There was a long silence. Then Tetsuo spoke.

"You talk awfully big for someone so little. Even if what you're saying is true, who are you to decide what makes a good leader? What do you do, Daichi Hara? I'll tell you what you do. You hang by your precious little garden all day and get pissed off whenever someone litters on it!"

A spark lit in Daichi's eyes.

"So…" he uttered venomously, "it was YOU!"

Tetsuo snickered nastily.

"What do you know about 'leading' people when all you have for friends are plants? You're a nobody, Daichi Hara. You act like you know everything about life, but really you're just a blowhard who talks out of his ass. You're all talk and no action. You bark, but you got no bite. A liar; that's all you are, Daichi. You've been lying your whole life; to your teachers, your friends… even yourself."

What happened next was so unexpected, not a sound was heard out of anyone. Not even the Taniguchis saw it coming when Daichi hurled his fist into Tetsuo's face.

Tetsuo stumbled back; then he smiled and threw a punch in return.

But Daichi caught his fist, much to everyone's surprise.

"No way!" Tetsuo exclaimed.

Daichi released Tetsuo's hand and retracted his arm, then delivered an uppercut, slugging him in the gut.

Tetsuo's eyes bulged like they were about to pop out of his head. He bent double, clutching his stomach with both hands, and fell to the floor with a grunt.

Toshio was the first to react. Ready to show off his wrestling skills, he seized Daichi by the shoulders and attempted to pin him against the ground. But then Daichi secured his hands around Toshio's waistline, hoisted him up, and hurtled him into the shoe lockers.

Onlookers dashed out of the way as Toshio's scrawny body crashed against the lockers, making a banging sound like someone slamming the drawer of a filing cabinet. Then Toshio fell with a thud and lay there limply, covering his hands over the fresh bruise on his head.

Tsuneo, baffled by his brothers' succumbing to Daichi's attacks, rushed forward and retracted his fist for a punch. He roared at the top of his lungs and swung his fist, but then Daichi stepped to the side and extended his leg, causing Tsuneo to trip and fall.

Tsuneo jumped to his feet and darted for him again. Then Daichi delivered a front kick to Tsuneo's face which sent him flying down the hallway. He landed on his backside and lay there motionless, out cold.

Mori, Haruka, and everyone else in the hallway gaped in astonishment.

Daichi looked around. Seeing the baffled, open mouthed faces of his peers felt unusual, yet satisfying. It was as if they were looking at him in a new light. However, he couldn't tell whether they were impressed, angry, or scared.

Discomforted by all the attention, Daichi walked over to Mori and nodded at her, indicating it was time to leave.

They started down the hallway; then a voice from behind called after them.

"Wait!"

They turned around. Tetsuo was on his feet, hunched over and still clutching his stomach.

"Where the hell did you learn to fight like that?" he asked Daichi through raspy grunts. "Last I remember you couldn't throw a punch to save your life!"

Daichi looked at Tetsuo and smiled.

"Sometimes you have to lose in order to win," he said simply.

With that, he turned around and headed down the hallway, Mori by his side.

As they neared the door, Mori leaned closer toward Daichi. Gently, she wrapped her arm around his and rested her head against his shoulder. Daichi smiled and placed his hand over hers, resting his head against her soft hair as they headed out the door.

Two minutes were left on the clock, the score tied at 75. Yagami's point guard attempted a shot; however, it was saved by Kurosaki's center Kyoya, who passed the ball to Akio the power forward.

Unfortunately, Akio wasn't as nimble as the others. Within seconds, he was overwhelmed at the midcourt line by Yagami's shooting guard, who stole the ball.

The Yagami shooting guard darted for the basket. But then, from out the corner of his eye, he saw a figure approaching. He attempted to alter direction, but it was too late. With the swift motion of Tsubaki's hand, the ball was stolen.

One minute left.

Tsubaki knew he had to do something fast. He was on the opposite side of the court, and five obstacles stood in his way from making a successful pass. He looked around to find a clear opening. On the left, Masaru was being blocked by Yagami's power forward, and on the right, Goro was being blocked by Yagami's point guard. Meanwhile, Yagami's center was guarding the basket, blocking Kyoya.

Left with no options, Tsubaki dashed along the right side of the court.

Yagami's point guard snickered and darted for Tsubaki.

Fool, he thought. *He wants to hog all the glory.*

Tsubaki signaled to Masaru, who responded by making his way toward the basket. But Tsubaki still couldn't make a clean pass. Yagami's power forward followed Masaru to the basket, blocking him along the way.

Tsubaki motioned with his hands, indicating he was about to make a pass.

What's he thinking? wondered Yagami's point guard as he closed in on Tsubaki. *There's no way he can make it to Masaru.*

But to his surprise, Tsubaki did not pass to Masaru. Instead, he passed it Akio, who was open on the left side.

What?! So Masaru was just a diversion!

Akio advanced down the court with a grin. The Yagami team lost all concern for him ever since he lost the ball, making him an opportune choice for a pass.

Thirty seconds left.

As a result of Tsubaki's cunning maneuver, all five Yagami players abandoned their positions and darted for Akio.

With one clear pathway between two of the approaching Yagami players, Akio brushed past them and threw the ball to Tsubaki, who had already reached the basket.

"He tricked us," muttered the Yagami point guard as Tsubaki leapt into the air, hurling the ball into the basket.

The score buzzer sounded off and the digital numbers on the scoreboard changed from 75 to 77 on the home side. The crowd roared with thunderous applause and the girls dashed onto the court, crowding around Tsubaki.

While the crowd filed out, Tsubaki chuckled playfully as the girls flooded him with compliments and date requests.

Then, from behind the girls' heads, Tsubaki spotted a lone figure standing in the bleachers, staring at him.

Tsubaki's face turned gravely serious when he recognized who it was. Moving with urgency, he pushed past the girls and approached the figure.

Tsubaki's observer was a handsome boy, thinly built and average height, only slightly older than he was. He wore a white doctor's jacket with a blue button down shirt underneath. He had clean-cut, neatly brushed black hair, and calm, alluring dark eyes which he wore glasses over. He stood there with his arms folded, smiling at Tsubaki.

"Not bad, Yunano," he said. "That was a clever move you made."

He spoke in a clear, articulate voice.

Tsubaki grabbed a towel from the bench and wiped his face.

"Thanks," Tsubaki responded flatly, sounding like he didn't want to speak to him. "So how's medical school, Ryozo?"

"Stupendous; I've passed all the exams with flying colors, and soon I'll be getting to do some hands on work."

"Ah. So… what are you doing here?"

"Just checking to see how my little brother's doing."

Tsubaki raised his eyebrows and frowned.

"Alright, alright," Ryozo said, rolling his eyes. "You want the truth? Fine; I stopped by to see if you've decided to do something more productive with your time, but... I see you're still playing games."

Tsubaki threw the towel around his neck and sighed.

"You seriously think I'm going to give up basketball? Come on, Ryozo. You're smarter than that."

"Yunano, how much longer are you going to keep this fantasy of yours going? It's time to wake up. Why don't you come back to our family, so you can make a name for yourself like the rest of us?"

"I appreciate your concern, Ryozo, but from now on, I'm going to do things my way. I don't care what dad thinks, nor Keijiro, Michiro, or you for that matter. Now if you'll excuse me, I'm going to go change. If you'd like, you can come see us play at the Interhigh Championship."

He turned around and headed for the locker room without a glance.

"You're being childish!" shouted Ryozo.

Tsubaki whipped around to see Ryozo glaring at him resentfully, eyebrows crossed and fists clenched.

"Let me put it to you straight, Yunano. Basketball will get you *nowhere* in life."

"What if I become pro?" Tsubaki retorted. "What then? Will I still be nowhere? I could make it big, you know."

"We both know what the chances are of that! Come on, Yunano. We're both smart, so let's not pretend like we're idiots. You have potential; potential to become something great. You…"

Ryozo bit his lip and hesitated.

"You have the potential…" he muttered begrudgingly, "to outclass all of us."

Tsubaki was taken aback by this.

"Dad always had high expectations for us," Ryozo continued, "so why don't you make him proud by making use of your talents?"

"He may have had high expectations, but he made it perfectly clear that if you want something, you have to earn it yourself. And that's exactly I'm going to do. Just you wait, Ryozo. One day, I will make a name for myself; but I'll make it doing what I love, not doing what dad wants."

He turned around and walked away, leaving Ryozo standing there alone in the quiet gymnasium.

Outside, the sun was setting, casting an orange glow over the school, reflecting bright gold off the windows.

The students filed out from the rear of the building following the basketball game. Meanwhile, at the front of the school, a mass of schoolgirls had crowded around a sleek black limousine parked by the entrance, and leaning against the limousine was a dashing young man with long, flowing black hair, dressed in a gray business suit. He was twenty-three years old, 6'1 tall, and athletically built with square pecs and broad shoulders. But what the girls loved most about him was his smile.

He had a manly face; firmly structured with a masculine jawline, and clean shaven with no taints or blemishes. When he smiled, his mouth revealed a full set of gleaming white teeth. And while he knew the girls surrounding him were far too young for his age, he humored them with his prince-like smile, which was all it took to satisfy them.

Over by the building, the entrance doors swung open and Ryozo stepped out. He stifled a laugh at the sight of his brother once again unable to avoid the attention of women. He walked over to the limousine and opened the door.

"So," said Michiro in his warm, smooth voice, "how'd it go?"

Ryozo didn't respond. He frowned glumly and stepped into the car without looking at his brother.

"I see," Michiro nodded. "So, Yunano still has his head in the clouds."

Michiro spoke with a gentle softness in his voice, as if he were wooing the girl of his dreams.

He stepped into the limousine and sat down next to his brother; then he shut the door and the limousine drove away.

Ryozo frowned as he stared out the window, watching the rows of cherry blossom trees whiz by.

Michiro patted his brother on the shoulder.

"Come now, Ryozo," he said with a smile. "Cheer up."

Ryozo made no form of response; he just continued staring.

Michiro raised his eyebrows and frowned.

"Don't look so crestfallen," he said. "Yunano was always like this, even as a child; stubborn, narrow-minded, always wanting to do things his way. That's Yunano for you. It's best if we just leave him to his ways."

Ryozo sat up in seat and turned to look at his brother.

"How could you say that?" he exclaimed. "Even if he is only our half-brother, we can't just abandon him! If he keeps this up, he'll fall right on his face."

"Yunano abandoned *us*, Ryozo. Or have you forgotten? Besides, we don't know that he'll fall on his face for sure."

"What're you saying? You don't seriously think he's going to make it in basketball, do you?"

"No matter how much we disapprove of it, one fact still remains. He's a Tsubaki, and a Tsubaki works endlessly to achieve what he desires. We mustn't undermine him so much because of his choices; he's intelligent and full of determination. There's no doubt in my mind that he could become the best basketball player in Japan."

"You almost sound like you're defending him."

"I disapprove of it just as much as you do, and I think he's wasting his abilities. But in my profession, sometimes we lawyers must wait and see how things play out. And that is what we must do with Yunano."

Ryozo didn't respond. He looked out the window again and sighed. The limousine was pulling up toward their house.

The Tsubakis' home was a large, ornate mansion that looked like two square prisms placed together by the corners. The exterior walls were paper-white and its two pyramid-shaped rooftops were velvet red. On the top floor, a line of windows encompassed the entire house, and on the side was a garage large enough to fit three cars.

When Ryozo and Michiro stepped out of the limousine, they noticed a silver car parked in their driveway.

"Huh," said Michiro as he tipped the limo driver. "Keijiro's back early from his meeting."

Ryozo and Michiro walked across their freshly cut lawn and stepped into the house. After taking their shoes off in the foyer, they walked up the grand staircase; a wide ascension of steps that broke off into two staircases halfway up. They took the right way up to the second floor where their older brother's office was located.

Just as they expected, they found their eldest sibling sitting at his desk, typing away at his laptop rapidly.

Not having noticed their presence yet, Ryozo decided to play a trick on his brother. He tiptoed up to him, grabbed him by his sides, and tickled him whilst shouting "BANZAI, BROTHA!" at the top of his lungs.

Keijiro jumped in his seat, yelping like a Chihuahua, and collapsed from his chair.

Michiro, who hung back by the door, covered his mouth and turned away, suppressing his laughter.

Keijiro rose to his feet and glared at his brothers solemnly.

"I swear," he grumbled, brushing off his black business suit. "You two still behave like children."

The eldest son of Kojiro Tsubaki was a professionally dressed young man with long, silky black hair tied back into a ponytail that ran all the way down his back. His appearance was strikingly similar to his youngest brother Yunano, with his smooth jawline and constant serious demeanor. Only Keijiro was fully matured, being twenty-six years old and 6'3 tall with broad shoulders and a prominent collarbone.

"Oh, lighten up, Mr. Serious," Ryozo teased.

"So," said Michiro, "what are you doing home so early? Dad cut the meeting short?"

"No, he's running it alone tonight," said Keijiro, straightening his tie and fixing his glasses. "He said it was a matter that didn't concern my division, so he relieved me. By the way, where have you two been?"

"Umm," Ryozo began, his eyes drifting toward Michiro.

Keijiro narrowed his eyes and grimaced in disgust.

"Don't tell me you're still bothering with *him* now are you?"

Ryozo looked down, guilt-stricken, and avoided his brother's cold gaze.

"Why?" Keijiro asked loudly. "I told you to stop bothering with that nuisance a long time ago!"

"Brother," Michiro interjected. "Stop trying to

sound like father. Where's the harm in what Ryozo did?"

"Oh, and I'm guessing *you're* the one who brought him there. You suckered up to the defensive side just like you always do, brother."

Michiro narrowed his eyes and glared at his brother.

"I might as well sound like father," Keijiro pressed on. "After all, he's too busy to deal with such petty affairs. I thought he made it perfectly clear the moment that little piece of trash walked out on us; we leave him be until he learns his lesson."

Keijiro stalked back to his desk and resumed typing.

"Although," he muttered to himself, "in my opinion, father was being too nice. I say we let him fend for himself. That is what he wanted, after all. But when his world comes crashing down, he better not come crying to us for help… because we won't give him any."

His robotic-like keystrokes were suddenly interrupted when Ryozo slammed the laptop shut, almost crushing Keijiro's hands.

Keijiro sat there staring blankly at his laptop, trying to comprehend what just happened. Then slowly, he turned his head in a reptilian-like manner to look at his brother, a baffled look in his eyes as if this were the first time he'd ever been disrespected.

"Don't you care?!" shouted Ryozo, his hand still over the laptop. "He's your brother! No; he's *our* brother! What gives you the right to decide his fate?!

He's still part of this family whether you like it or not!"

Keijiro rose from his chair and clenched his fist, glaring at his brother indignantly. But then his expression eased and his hand relaxed. He fixed his glasses and sighed.

"You're quite right, Ryozo," he said calmly. "Yunano's one of us, and there's nothing I can do to change that. Whatever father decides on his fate is the final verdict. I'm sorry, brother. I guess I've been so infuriated by his self-exile that I turned a blind eye to his tragic past."

"Tragic past?" asked Ryozo.

"Oh yes," nodded Keijiro, sitting down. "I'm assuming father never told you the *whole* story as to how Yunano was born."

Ryozo thought on it for a moment.

"Whenever I approached father about it," he said, sounding like he was uncovering a mystery, "he always tried backing out of the conversation, or avoiding the topic altogether. However, there was one time when I asked him who Yunano's mom was and what happened to her. All he told me was that she was an old friend of his, and he never found out he was the father until she revealed it in her will. I know she died when Yunano was two years old, but other than that, that's all I know."

Keijiro and Michiro looked at each other and nodded.

"I see," said Keijiro. "Well, while that's true, vague as it is, there's much more to it than that. You see, dad knew he was the father long before he ever read the will."

Ryozo sat up in his chair and looked his brother in the eye.

"Tell me," he said seriously. "Tell me everything."

Keijiro fixed his glasses and sat back in his chair.

"It all started seventeen years ago," he began. "You weren't even a year old yet. I was nine years old at the time, and I remember it all very clearly. Father was under a lot of stress; the Hanaoka Corporation was suffering from a terrible economic recession that year. When I became the Vice President of the company, I was told more about that year by the senior members of the business, and it turns out the total gross profits made that year were only a fourth of what we made last year."

Ryozo widened his eyes in astonishment.

"I was only six at the time," Michiro added. "But I'll never forget the look on dad's face. Every day that year, he came home looking tired and annoyed, like he hated everyone in the world. Gradually, it got worse and worse. Some nights he came home with bags under his eyes, looking like he hadn't slept in a week."

"I remember that too," said Keijiro. "That was because father *didn't* sleep for weeks. With the employment rate down and the economy in the toilet, father was forced to lay off a considerable amount of the company's employees. He had no choice; it was the only way he could keep the company on its feet. Unfortunately, as a result, he had to arrive at work earlier and leave even later. And Mother was facing problems of her own. She, like many others, was laid off that year. Now that I think back on it, I understand more now why mother and father fought so much. With mother scraping for jobs while taking care of three children, and father working ridiculous hours, not making nearly as much as he usually made, the two of them of together was a bad mix. It was clear their marriage was headed downhill."

"Was that really all it took for mom and dad to split up?" asked Ryozo.

"It may not sound like much, but trust me; when the world turns to shit, and you have to work so hard that you have no time to spend with your wife and kids, then what's the point in remaining a family? I don't mean to sound cold, but with the way their situation was at the time, I think divorce was the best option. Anyway, mother and father got divorced, and the three of us were left in father's custody, since he made the most affordable living. Unfortunately, that only made things harder for him. Without the aid of mother's income, he was forced to work even longer hours. However, even as he trudged through those grim, dreary days, there was one thing that kept him going."

"And what was that?" asked Ryozo.

"Her name was Satomi; Satomi Fujihara. Every morning, father would walk through the entrance doors, only to be greeted by the cheerful 'good morning' of the pretty secretary at the front desk, Satomi Fujihara. For a while, that's all it was. But soon, as the number of employees decreased, and as our family fell apart, father and this woman developed a closer kind of friendship. Their simple 'hellos' and 'good mornings' became full-on conversations. Every evening, before they locked up, father and Satomi would have long talks about life and how things were going.

"I remember the first time I saw her. It was father's day off and we were downtown. He picked me up from school, then we stopped by the company building so he could grab some important papers. He only meant for it to be a quick stop, but we didn't leave until a half hour later. I remember getting bored and impatient because father spent so much time talking to the woman at the front desk.

"She was a lovely woman; very cheerful. I think Satomi grew on him after a while. In fact, I'd say she was the only person who father felt he could truly open up to. Now, I don't know when it occurred, but at some point, father and Satomi had an affair, and together, they conceived Yunano. When Satomi told father about her pregnancy, she said she'd provide for the child alone, because she didn't want to be a burden to him. But Father cared deeply for her, and despite his numerous offers to help, she declined every one of them. He even offered for her to come live with us, but she refused, because she knew it would've been awkward for the three of us. So they went their separate ways.

"When father came into work the next day, she wasn't at the front desk. It turned out that she quit her job at the company and got hired elsewhere. Nine months later, she gave birth to Yunano, and she spent a whole year raising the child on her own. By the time the year had passed, she was diagnosed with breast cancer, and the doctors told her it had already reached stage 3. When she asked how much time she had left, they said six months to a year."

Ryozo lowered his head, a pitiful gleam in his eyes.

"The same time she was diagnosed," Keijiro continued, "the economy had stabilized, and the Hanaoka Corporation returned to its former glory. Father rejoiced in seeing his business thrive again. Then he received the call from Satomi. She told him how long she had, and asked for him to take care of Yunano once she was gone. Father immediately responded by getting her the best cancer treatment possible and having her move into the mansion with us. When she moved in, it was really awkward, especially for me and Michiro. We were angry and jealous. Father spent so much time tending to Satomi and Yunano, we felt like we had been forgotten."

"I had a bad outburst one time," said Michiro. "One day, I got really mad at dad and I yelled at him, accusing him for replacing mom with this total stranger and neglecting the three of us all the time."

Keijiro nodded solemnly, recalling the memory.

"We were young and naïve; too young to understand. But as time went on, we warmed up to Satomi. As we watched her body deteriorate, we became more sympathetic of her situation. Her body became thin and frail, and her skin turned pale white. Her head became bald from the treatment and her breasts sagged, signifying she was nearing the end.

"When she died, I didn't know what to feel. Part of me felt relieved that her suffering was over. However, another part of me felt sad. She spent an entire year living with us, and even though we were unaccepting at first, Satomi became like a second mother to us once we got to know her.

"I remember one time when the four of us all played together in her room. I'll never forget the look on her face that day. I remember laughing hysterically; you, me and Michiro having fun with our new baby brother. That was when I looked up at Satomi, who lay in bed giggling happily at the four us. Then she looked directly at me, and she smiled with a proud look in her eyes. I smiled back at her, but then, she started to tear up. I walked to her bedside and handed her a tissue.

"'Satomi,' I said. 'What's the matter?'

"She wiped away her tears and looked at me again.

"'Nothing,' she said, still smiling. 'It's just... I'm glad to see you're all having fun together. I wish it could be like this forever.'

"I looked at my brothers and chuckled. I understood what she meant.

"'Keijiro,' I heard her say.

"I turned to look at her, and she was holding her hand out to me. Carefully, I took her hand and listened closely, for what she said next truly struck at my heart.

"'I know I'm not you're mother,' she said. 'But the three of you are the brothers of my son, which means I care for you just as equally. When I'm gone, please look after my son. Can you do that for me, Keijiro?'

"At that moment, I made a promise to her; that I'd watch over Yunano, and wherever he'd go, I'd make sure to lead him in the right direction like a good big brother. So to answer your question, Ryozo, yes; I do care about Yunano. Though, I do resent him for abandoning us so he could throw his life away."

Keijiro sighed and fixed his glasses.

"I want to see him succeed like the rest of us, but the longer we let him keep this up, the more it feels like I'm breaking my promise."

As the orange glow of the sunset washed over Tokyo, Tsubaki walked home down the sidewalk of Shinjuku with his sports bag slung over his shoulder. He stepped with an annoyance in his stride, a tired, grouchy look on his face.

"Damn Ryozo," he muttered. "When're they going to learn that what they want me to do isn't what I want to do? I'll show them. One day, I'll be the one on top, and *I'll* be the one they'll look up to."

Tsubaki stopped suddenly. Out of the corner of his eye, he saw something quite disturbing.

He turned his head and when he looked down the dark alleyway, he saw a vague silhouette in the shadows sitting on the ground, its back against the wall.

266

Tsubaki started down the alleyway and approached the figure. Once he got a good view of what was there, he stopped and gasped, stumbling back.

It was a man; a tall young man with singed wavy blond hair, dressed in a bloodstained white poet shirt and ripped blue jeans with bits of bloody skin protruding from the tears. He had a gloomy, tired expression on his ash-ridden face, looking down glumly. But what frightened Tsubaki the most was the man's right arm, which dangled from his shoulder, held together by a braid of veins.

The man lifted his head slowly. Then his eyes met with Tsubaki and he chuckled.

"You mind giving me a hand, kid?" the man spoke. "Hehe, get it? Cause of my… oh. Well I guess it's really an arm, but… whatever; you know what I mean."

He spoke with a German accent.

The man let out a faint, breathy chuckle. Then his eyelids fluttered and he went unconscious.

18 — FIRST BLOOD

Inside the penthouse of the Kanemochi no Hotel, Maddox summoned a white flame ball around himself. It began to spin, causing the entire room to shake violently. Its brightness was so intense that even as Mirko shielded his eyes, the light shining through the creases between his fingers blinded him.

Mirko eased back toward the window. He tried coming up with a method of escape, but then he remembered what Daichi had done to him, and how his powers were draining. Even if he did have any power left, Mirko knew it wouldn't be enough to get him out of the building, or to beat Maddox. All he could do was stand there, and as he watched Daichi fly out of the floor and over his head with Mori in his arms, he finally came to the realization that his plan had failed, and there was nothing he could do now.

The flame ball whirled faster and faster, until suddenly it stopped and shrunk down, levitating between Maddox's hands.

Everything was silent now. Not even the sounds of the raindrops were audible. Mirko gasped, but he couldn't breathe. Then he realized that the white orb had consumed all the oxygen inside the penthouse, so as to maintain stability.

Maddox stood there calmly with his eyes closed, holding the flame ball between his hands; then he opened his fingers, and in less than a millisecond, the flame ball released itself and expanded, resulting in a massive explosion.

All Mirko heard was a loud bang, and then, everything around him turned bright white. Maddox, the walls of the hotel, the floor beneath his feet; it all disappeared, leaving Mirko floating in a void of nothingness.

So, thought Mirko. *Is this what it's like to die? It doesn't feel like much. If that's all there is, why does everyone make such a big fuss over it? It doesn't hurt. In fact, it's rather peaceful. Already I feel like I'm being welcomed into an angel's arms.*

Then Mirko was hit with the sharp, searing pain of

the flames. Suddenly, he could feel himself moving, like he was being propelled through the air by a gust of wind. The whiteness surrounding him became a wavering mix of orange and yellow, the heavy smell of smoke filling his nose.

Faster and faster his body hurtled through the air, the exterior of the hotel coming into view. Ablaze in flames, the penthouse resembled the top of a torch.

Mirko flailed his limbs, but when he did, it felt like he was being stabbed by a thousand knives. Through his scorched eyes, he could see his arms reddened, blistered by the heat of the flames.

"What the?!" Mirko gasped, looking out at the Tokyo skyline. "How the hell did I survive that?! I should've been turned to ash! The fact that I've only suffered third degree burns is a miracle!"

Mirko looked down; the streets of Shinjuku were drawing closer.

"*Scheisse,*" he grumbled. "This is going to hurt."

Mirko shifted the position of his body so that he was falling headfirst, aiming for an abandoned alleyway down below. He increased speed as he plummeted, his lips and eyelids flapping in the wind.

The concrete ground of the alleyway came closer into view. Then there was a loud crack, like the sound of a baseball hitting against a bat, and Mirko's head burst open like a watermelon. Gobs of brain, blood, and body fluid flew from his skull and splattered all over the walls of the alleyway. His head crushed against his neck, and his bones shattered upon impact. A sharp pain coursed through his nerves as his bones pierced through his skin, protruding outwards like a pincushion. At that moment, Mirko would've let out a bloodcurdling, "AGGHHH!" but he couldn't; not with his head in a million pieces.

Through his reddened eyeballs, which landed ten feet from his mangled carcass, Mirko could see down the alleyway, and to his luck, no one had appeared at the scene.

Dammit, this'll take an entire day to heal! Oh well, might as well get started with the process.

Through the night and over the course of the following day, Mirko's body formed back together. That afternoon, he reconstructed all of his bones. That night, he reattached most of his veins. And the next day, he returned his bones and organs to their correct positions, returning the blood to his arteries.

By late afternoon, Mirko had nearly finished regenerating, and the only part of his body left to reattach was his right arm.

Mirko sighed in relief.

"Once this is done, all that's left to do is wait for the burns to heal."

He looked down at his hands gloomily.

"Although, what's to celebrate when I can't even use my powers? For all I know, this effect on me could last forever, and if that's the case, then what's the point in living?"

He lowered his head and sulked while his veins gradually reconnected his arm.

Suddenly, he heard footsteps, but he didn't care.

He heard someone gasp and stumble back. He lifted his head and smiled at the handsome young man before him.

"You mind giving me a hand, kid?" he chuckled. "Hehe, get it? Cause of my… oh. Well I guess it's really an arm, but… whatever; you know what I mean."

Mirko, exhausted and not having slept in over a day, became drowsy. He drifted in and out of consciousness; then his eyelids fluttered, and the sight of the black-haired boy's horrified face was last thing he saw.

Mirko was no longer in the alleyway when he awoke. Instead, he opened his eyes to a white ceiling. He lifted his head and looked around. He was lying on a sofa inside an apartment he had never been in before. On the wall across from the sofa were two doorways on opposite sides. The left lead to the kitchen, while the right lead to a small hallway with two doors on either side; the bathroom to the left, and the bedroom to the right. Behind Mirko's head was the entrance door, and on the wall next to him was a poster of some orange-haired basketball player from an anime performing a slam dunk. Next to the poster was a single window; Mirko could see it was nighttime outside.

Against the wall to the right of the hallway was a work desk with a computer, and between the two doorways in the living room was a flat-screen television mounted on the center wall.

Two framed pictures hung on either side of the television. Mirko eyed them curiously. To the left was a photo of a high school basketball team. One of the players was the black-haired boy who he met in the alleyway. And to the right was a photo of a young black-haired woman sitting with her hands folded, a warm smile on her face.

Mirko heard the sound of water boiling in the kitchen. He looked over at the doorway, and then, the boy with the black hair stepped out, carrying a bowl of steaming ramen.

The boy raised his eyebrows at Mirko.

"Oh. You're up."

He walked over and placed the bowl on the coffee table in front of the sofa.

"Here," said the boy. "Eat up. You'll feel better."

Mirko sat up and stared blankly at the bowl of ramen like he didn't know what to do with it.

Tsubaki took it as a sign he didn't want to eat it.

"Suit yourself," he muttered, walking back into the kitchen.

Mirko sat there silently. Then he sat himself down on the floor, picked up the chopsticks, and lifted a clump of noodles into his mouth.

"What's the point?" Mirko sighed. "It's not like starvation can kill me. But then again, the feeling of not having something in your belly is quite discomforting. Well, I guess I might as well nourish myself while I can."

He took another mouthful. Then Tsubaki reentered the living room, carrying another bowl. He sat himself down on the opposite side of the coffee table and proceeded to eat his ramen.

The two of them ate in silence for about a minute. Then Tsubaki spoke.

"By the way, the name's Yunano; Yunano Tsubaki."

"Mirko Fleischer," said Mirko through a mouthful of noodles. "It's a pleasure. So, Yunano Tsubaki, how did I end up in this fine home of yours?"

"As soon as you passed out, I brought you here. It was clear you needed immediate treatment, and I couldn't just stand there and watch someone die. You looked like Death when I found you. It's a good thing it was me who stumbled upon you that alleyway. Had it been anyone else, they probably would've just panicked. Though, I'll admit; you had me afraid for a while. Your burns were pretty severe, and as for your arm, I was almost tempted to amputate it. But when I returned from the pharmacy after purchasing extra bandages, all your burns had healed, and your arm looked as good as new. Even the singed bits of your hair returned to normal…"

Mirko looked up at Tsubaki and chuckled.

"Ah, yes. Well, luckily, my body's very responsive with injuries. I've experienced so many of them in my lifetime, I guess you could say my body's grown used to it."

Tsubaki narrowed his eyes and stared at Mirko suspiciously, knowing there had to be more to his explanation.

"Is that woman your mother?" Mirko asked, indicating the photo of the young woman. "She looks kind," was the best compliment he could muster.

"Yeah," Tsubaki responded flatly. "I don't remember much about her. She died of cancer when I was only two."

"Shame," said Mirko.

He made it sound like a simple inconvenience.

"What about the rest of your family?" Mirko continued. "Aren't you a little young to be living on your own?"

"I had a falling out with my father."

"I see. Family problems?"

"I'd rather not talk about it."

Tsubaki looked away and stared solemnly at the floor. There was a long silence. Then he looked at Mirko again.

"So," he said, returning to the subject at hand. "Back in the alleyway, did someone do that to you?"

"Not exactly."

"Then how did you get those burns? Were you caught in an explosion?"

"Kind of."

"And what about your arm? Did you fall off a building or something?"

Mirko rose to his feet and lay down on the couch, an irritated scowl ridding his face.

"I'd rather not talk about it," he grumbled, rolling to his side.

Tsubaki frowned disappointedly and rose to his feet, picking up his empty bowl and heading back into the kitchen.

Mirko spoke no more after that.

Daichi and Mori walked home together after the game. By the time they reached Mori's house, it was nighttime, and all was quiet in the neighborhood.

"Well," said Daichi, "goodnight, Mori. I'll see you at school tomorrow."

As Daichi began to walk away, he heard Mori's voice behind him.

"Daichi…"

He turned around to see Mori smiling at him, a gleam in her eyes.

"Good job today. You showed those Taniguchis what for."

Daichi chuckled modestly.

"I just landed a few lucky hits. It was nothing really."

"No, Daichi," said Mori, walking closer.

She rested her arms on Daichi's shoulders and leaned in close, gazing deeply into his eyes.

"That wasn't just luck," she continued in a soft tone. "That was bravery. It took courage to do what you did back there. And for that, I'm proud of you; truly."

She closed her eyes and leaned in closer. Just as her lips were about to touch his, Daichi stumbled back and chuckled awkwardly, his face bright red.

"Ah, yes!" he exclaimed, talking fast. "Yes, yes, yes! True bravery indeed! You're right on that one, Mori! Well, it's getting late, so, I think I'll head home now. Bye!"

He dashed away at an impressive speed and was lost from view.

Mori stood there, baffled. Then she smiled and walked up to her house, giggling to herself along the way.

Meanwhile, Daichi had reached his house. He walked across the pathway, and when he opened the door, he gasped in alarm.

Sitting there on the living room couch, his feet up on the coffee table, was Maddox. His head was turned toward the doorway, as if he were expecting him. He had a serious look on his face.

"Jeez!" said Daichi. "You scared me. What are you doing here, anyway?"

"Daichi," said Maddox in a solemn tone, "it's more than halfway through the month, and you're still a thousand kills short on your quota."

"Maddox, can we not talk about this now? Besides, we still need to talk about what happened to me at the hotel; how I healed myself, how I healed you, and how I severed the connection between Mirko and his powers. At first, I didn't remember any of it, but after I went to bed that night, visions flashed through my head. I saw two energy orbs; one white one and one black. Then I woke up and I lost the image. Last night, there were even more visions. I remember seeing Kasami's body flying through the air, then the surprised look on Mirko's face when I entered the penthouse. What happened to me, Maddox? Was that even me?"

"I'm not sure," he said, rising to his feet. "I have no

idea what it was. However, I can assure you that it has no affiliation with your Death powers. It was all very strange; I hadn't seen anything like it since…"

Maddox stopped mid-sentence and gasped, his eyes widening in realization.

"Wait, that's it!" he exclaimed.

"What's it?"

"I remember now. I think I know why you have these powers, Daichi. I'm not sure what they are, but I think it has something to do with your father."

"Really?!" asked Daichi excitedly. "Well go on, tell me!"

"I will, but now is not the time. First, we need to take care of that gap in your kill count."

Daichi looked away and grimaced.

"Come now," said Maddox sternly. "You knew it would come to this eventually. How long did you think you could put it off? It's the only way to continue living, Daichi; unless you'd rather die."

"No!" shouted Daichi. "… Fine then," he grumbled. "So how am I supposed to go about this?"

"Follow me."

Maddox grabbed Daichi by his shoulder and hauled him toward the doorway.

"Hold up!" Daichi protested. "Where are we going?"

"You'll see," said Maddox as he lead him out the door.

Back at the apartment, Mirko was sitting on the couch, watching an anime on television.

"Seriously?!" Mirko laughed aloud. "Cards that summon monsters? There's no way that could happen in real life."

While Mirko was wrapped up in his show, Tsubaki sat down at his computer and began surfing the news, skimming for articles about the Kanemochi no Hotel incident and the kidnapping of the Chief's daughter.

"Hmm," muttered Tsubaki to himself. "That's odd. They weren't able to apprehend any of the kidnappers. I wonder…"

His eyes drifted to Mirko, who flung his hands in the air.

"Are you shitting me?!" exclaimed Mirko. "That Kaiba prick stole the Blue-Eyes White Dragon from Yugi's grandfather! That was dirty! Although, I guess I'm one to talk."

Ever since Tsubaki found Mirko in the alleyway, he had a faint suspicion that he was the one who kidnapped Mori, and as he dug deeper through the news articles, his suspicions were furthered.

It's all coming together now, thought Tsubaki. *The alleyway where I found Mirko was only four blocks away from the Kanemochi no Hotel. And that grumpy mood of his; it's like he's mad about something. Perhaps over losing his hostage? And those injuries; it's likely he suffered them from the fiasco at the Hotel.*

"Hey!" bellowed Mirko.

Tsubaki whipped his head around in alarm, but it was just Mirko yelling at the television.

"This Pegasus guy is awesome!" Mirko continued.

279

"He's the only bad guy in this show with a brain!… I wish I had his hair."

Tsubaki narrowed his eyes and scowled.

There's something else though. Those triangles on his face; I think I've seen them before. That's right! When I saw Daichi in downtown Shinjuku the morning Mori was kidnapped! He had a triangle on his face, and so did the guy who was with him. Could it be that Daichi was involved in the kidnapping? No; he'd never do something like that. Not to Mori. But then… what are those triangles, and what do they mean?

Tsubaki eyed Mirko suspiciously.

Just who are you, Mirko Fleischer? More importantly, what are you?

"You know what, Tsubaki?" giggled Mirko. "You remind me of Kaiba."

Maddox and Daichi walked along the neon-lit streets of Tokyo until they reached the train station. As they boarded the train, Daichi asked Maddox where they were going. But Maddox didn't answer. A few minutes later, when the train reached the halfway point, Maddox pointed out the window and said, "There is our destination."

Daichi turned his head and looked out the window. There, looming in the distance was Mount Fuji; the wide, conical shaped volcano on Honshu Island that towered into the sky. In the night, it looked like the outline of a giant black wave rising in the air, ready to descend upon the city.

The train dropped them off near the foot of the

mountain. As they began their ascent, Daichi looked around and realized how dim the area was.

"You sure we don't need flashlights?" he asked. "I can't see a thing."

"Don't worry," Maddox chuckled. "We have all the light we need."

He held out his hand and ignited a flame in his palm; then he continued his way up the mountain, Daichi following behind. After five hours of climbing, Daichi and Maddox finally reached the peak of the mountain. When they reached the cliff, Daichi dropped to his knees and clutched his shoulders.

"It's freezing up here!" he complained, his teeth chattering.

"Come on," said Maddox, walking over to the edge of the cliff. "Now is not the time to rest. Now is the time to kill."

"Jeez, you sound more cold-hearted than Mirko."

"Don't compare me to him!" shouted Maddox, turning his head. "Don't ever compare me to him. Understand?"

"Sure," muttered Daichi.

"Good. Now come on. We don't have all night."

Reluctantly, Daichi walked to edge of the cliff. He stopped next to Maddox and gazed upon the illuminated skyline of Tokyo that stretched all the way into the distance, the cool wind blowing against his hair.

"Now," said Maddox, "do you remember the earthquake you created back at the hotel?"

Daichi nodded silently.

"Alright then. Now, unleash your powers and focus all your energy onto yourself. Then, once you feel ready, let go. Once you do that, your powers will release a seismic wave."

Daichi gulped; then he closed his eyes and took a deep breath.

"Alright," he said, opening his eyes. "I'm ready."

Maddox nodded, then stepped back. All was quiet now; so quiet that all you could hear was the howl of the wind thrashing against the mountain rocks.

Daichi clenched his fists and his green aura ignited, surrounding his body and beaming intensely like a wild flame. With each passing second, the aura grew larger. Then Daichi sighed and the aura condensed.

"No!" shouted Maddox. "Not yet, Daichi! Just concentrate your energy onto yourself! I'll tell you when to let go."

Heeding Maddox's command, Daichi took a deep breath and the aura grew larger again, illuminating the entire top of the mountain.

Well, Yoshito, thought Maddox, *he truly is your son.*

Back at the apartment, Mirko sat absorbed in his anime, until suddenly, Tsubuki grabbed the remote and clicked off the television.

"Hey!" barked Mirko. "Turn that back on! I was right in the middle of the Battle City Arc!"

"Shut up," snapped Tsubaki. "Listen, you can play it cool all you want, but I know you're hiding something."

"Don't we all have something to hide?" Mirko asked snidely, smiling at him.

"The Kanemochi no Hotel," Tsubaki pressed on. "Does that ring a bell?"

Mirko frowned, glaring at him.

"Thought so," said Tsubaki. "Tell me; how did you survive that explosion?"

Mirko stayed silent.

"Are you the one who kidnapped Mori?"

Mirko turned away from Tsubaki and remained silent, a disgusted look on his face.

"Dammit," grumbled Tsubaki.

He stalked off into his bedroom. Then a minute later, he came back out dressed in running gear.

"Where are you going?" asked Mirko quietly.

"I'm taking my run up to Mount Fuji."

"Isn't it a little late?"

"I need some fresh air, and some time to think."

With that, he stalked out of the apartment and headed for the train station. After the train dropped him off, he spent the next five hours running up the mountain.

However, when he reached the peak, he was welcomed to a strange sight. Standing at the edge of the cliff was Daichi, and behind him was the same man he saw with him in the city.

Tsubaki darted behind a large rock and hid there, watching in silence.

Daichi? What the hell is he doing here?

His thoughts were interrupted when a jet of green light burst out of nowhere, illuminating the peak of the mountain. As he shielded his eyes, Tsubaki noticed the light was giving off from where Daichi stood.

The light started to fade; Tsubaki lowered his hand to get a better look. The light was surrounding Daichi, like an aura of some sort.

"No!" shouted the man. "Not yet, Daichi! Just concentrate your energy onto yourself! I'll tell you when to let go."

What the hell is he talking about? Is this a science experiment of some sort, or... could this be something from beyond this world?

The aura became brighter, giving off an energy so strong that Tsubaki could feel a vibration in the ground.

"Just a little more!" shouted Maddox.

The aura had risen nearly fifty feet into the air, glowing so bright, Daichi's figure was no longer visible.

"Ready..." Maddox began.

"NO!" Tsubaki shouted, but his voice was lost through the overwhelming force of the aura.

"Now!" bellowed Maddox.

Everything went silent. The howl of the wind was absent; not even the sound of their breath was heard as Daichi's aura condensed into a dim illumination.

Then Daichi roared at the top of his lungs and his aura released a wave of energy which shot through the air and disappeared into the distance. Immediately afterwards, a strong seismic wave was released from beneath Daichi's feet. It shot through the ground all the way down the mountain, creating an avalanche like a wave in the ocean. The tremor traveled northeast, reaching the city of Tokyo. Within seconds, numerous structures were demolished, ranging from small residential homes to well-built skyscrapers. A total of three skyscrapers collapsed as a result of the earthquake. Two in the Shibuya district, and one in Shinjuku; the one in Shinjuku being none other than the already damaged Kanemochi no Hotel. Its collapse caused a considerable amount of deaths in the area; primarily to those who were in close proximity as it came down.

Meanwhile, inside Tsubaki's apartment, Mirko sat back on the couch and sniggered as he stared up at the quivering ceiling, bits of rubble falling on his face.

"Well, well," he said amusedly, "looks like he's getting his first kills."

Back on the mountain, Daichi blinked, and the earthquake was over.

What lay before him was a tragic sight. Several buildings in Tokyo he recognized were gone now. Smoke rose into the sky from several areas, and many of the skyscrapers looked off-center and damaged, like they were missing glass. But the worst part was that from where he stood, he could hear the faint cries of citizens struggling to free themselves from beneath the fallen debris.

"Oh my god," Daichi gasped emptily. "What have I done?"

Maddox stepped closer. When he saw the horrified look on Daichi's face, he placed his hand on his shoulder and said, "Calm down. You did what you had to do. It's over now."

"No," Daichi muttered, staring into his trembling hands with wide eyes. "I killed them. All those innocent people… I – I killed them!"

Maddox grabbed Daichi by his shoulders and gave him a rough shake.

"Daichi, you need to get a grip. If you don't, the pain's just going to eat at you."

"I CAN'T" he bellowed.

Amidst his pity and self-loathing, Daichi brushed Maddox's hands away and bolted for the cliff. Just as he was about to jump off, Maddox caught him by his shirt and yanked him back.

"What the hell are you doing?!" shouted Maddox, seizing Daichi by his shoulders. "That wouldn't kill you anyway! Did you really think you could escape this job that easily? It's not that simple!"

"Then you kill me, Maddox!"

Maddox gasped and stepped back.

"What did you say?" he muttered.

"You heard me," Daichi repeated. "If I can't do it myself, then it might as well be you. Go ahead, Maddox; earn yourself a kill. You've been around for a hundred years. You can handle it. I can't."

"Yes you can," said Maddox calmly. "You just don't know it yet. I've managed to keep myself alive all this time, and you know how I did it? 1,080,000 lives. A kill short and I'd be dead by now."

"That's you, Maddox. That's not me. I don't want

to keep doing this. Sacrificing other people's lives for my own, it's despicable. Besides, what if I become so comfortable with killing that I end up like Mirko? I don't want that to happen, Maddox. Those people who died out there were innocent; they deserved to live. Is my life really worth all the bodies beneath that rubble?"

For a moment, Maddox didn't respond. Then he looked out into the distance with a nostalgic look in his eyes and said, "You know, I used to think just like you back then. For a while, I hated my powers, and I would've liked nothing more than to kill myself, so as to spare mankind. But then I remembered my parents and what my father said. He always taught me to live; to stay strong no matter how many obstacles stood in my way. Once I remembered his words, I realized that if I let these powers keep bringing me down, I'll never be happy. That's why I decided to kill criminals, so I could use my powers to do some good in this world."

"Even so, it still doesn't excuse the fact that you're killing people."

"Daichi," said Maddox calmly, "you know how your father went about his kills?"

Daichi's expression eased.

"He would visit terminally ill hospital patients in their rooms and ask them if they'd like to die. Having suffered enough, most of them said yes. And that's how he racked up his kills; a simple, but effective method. I always admired your father for that. He found a way to kill innocent people without pain or heartbreak. So you see, Daichi, killing the innocent doesn't mean you have to be brutal. Us humans, we're all meant to die someday."

Daichi stood there in silence for a moment, moved by Maddox's words. Then, the terror-stricken look vanished from his face and he looked up at Maddox with a glint of hope in his eyes.

"Right," he said. "If my father found a way to live, then so can I."

Maddox smiled and placed his hand on Daichi's shoulder.

"Look," he said, pointing into the distance beyond the city. "The sun's about to rise."

As the sun's golden glow broke from behind the Tokyo skyline, Tsubaki sprinted down the mountain back to the city, a stream of thoughts racing through his mind.

Daichi, he thought, running through the debris-ridden streets. *He caused this! Wait… those triangles! I knew they meant something. Daichi, the man with him, Mirko, they all must possess this… power.*

After passing through the mountains of wreckage, the haunting cries of families struggling to free themselves filling his ears, Tsubaki finally arrived at the apartment complex, which survived from the earthquake. He ran up the stairs and burst open the door.

Mirko, who sat on the couch watching TV, turned his head in alarm.

"Ah," he said pleasantly. "You've returned. So, how was your midnight outing?"

"Listen," said Tsubaki firmly. "I don't care who you are or what your motives are. I just watched my best friend kill a thousand people by causing an earthquake on top of Mount Fuji."

Mirko raised his eyebrows and stood up, a devious smirk forming across his face.

"There's no telling whether he might do that again," Tsubaki continued. "And I'm not willing to risk that chance. So please; all I ask is for you to show me how I can obtain these powers for myself, so I can stop him from hurting anyone else."

Mirko rubbed the stubble of his chin and snickered mischievously.

My my, he thought. *This should be interesting.*

On the peak of Mount Fuji, Daichi and Maddox stood side by side at the edge of the cliff, watching the sun blaze bright pink across the clear morning sky.

"So," said Maddox. "How do you feel now?"

"I don't know how to explain it," said Daichi, touching the triangle beneath his eye. "I guess… stabilized, like something inside me was missing something, but now it's there."

"Hmm," nodded Maddox. "That means you've completed your quota for this month. Your death powers are no longer starving; they're full and enticed, for now at least."

Maddox looked over and noticed Daichi scrolling through his cell phone.

"What are you doing?" he asked, raising an eyebrow.

"I'm looking up how many people have been confirmed dead… about 1,260 so far."

"Ah, and that's only counting the Kanto region, correct?"

Daichi nodded.

"That earthquake was a strong one," Maddox continued. "I'm guessing about an 8.0 on the Richter scale."

"8.6," said Daichi.

"Wow," marveled Maddox. "Then I'm positive those numbers are still to grow; there's no telling how far your tremor might have reached."

Maddox looked over again and noticed Daichi still scrolling through his phone.

"What are you looking up now?" he asked.

"Obituaries on the victims who died from the earthquake. I want to know who I killed."

Maddox snatched the phone out of Daichi's hand and powered it off.

"Hey!" Daichi shouted. "What was that for?"

"It's best you don't know," said Maddox solemnly. "Once the faces of your victims are in your memory, it'll only make you feel worse. Believe me, I know. That's why I had you create a massive earthquake; so the connection between you and your victims is less personal."

Daichi was silent for a moment. Then he looked up at Maddox and asked, "Is this what it's going to be like for the rest of my life?"

Maddox sighed, then chuckled lightly.

"Come now, you knew that the moment you found out you were a Death."

Daichi's face turned grim.

Maddox placed his hand on his shoulder.

"Don't worry," he said comfortingly. "You have friends; people who you can count on. Be grateful for that, and enjoy their company while they last. I wasn't so lucky."

Daichi smiled at Maddox; then, as he looked out into the distance, shed a single tear which streaked over the black triangle beneath his eye.

That morning, Daichi understood what it meant to be a Death. And as he stood there, staring out into golden sunlight, he could already see the darkness of what was to come.

CPSIA information can be obtained
at www.ICGtesting.com
Printed in the USA
BVHW030218280119
538826BV00001B/142/P